The Heart of the Matter

Remo decided to use force. The blade was simpler.

"You're going to kill yourself with your own knife," Remo said softly. "Here we go."

He clasped the young man's hand around the knife so it could not let go and pressed it into the stomach, and, feeling the blade had a sharpness to it, he very slowly brought it up to where he felt the heart muscle throb against it.

"Oh, God," said the young man who knew now he was going to die and had not expected anything like that.

When the heart went, when the muscle was pierced and his blood flowed out of his stomach and now very fast out, all over the place, and he finally was able to let go of the knife because the guy was walking up on the street, then it dawned on the young man, in the final clarity of the last moment of life, even a seventeen-year-old life, that this guy he had planned to stick had snuffed out his life without missing one step.

The city was dark and Remo moved on. There was some blood on his left thumb and he flicked it off.

THE DESTROYER by Warren Murphy & Richard Sapir

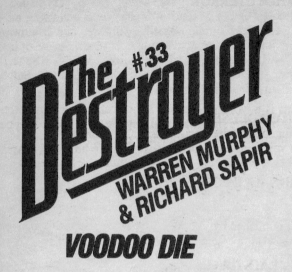

The Destroyer #33

WARREN MURPHY & RICHARD SAPIR

VOODOO DIE

PINNACLE BOOKS
WINDSOR PUBLISHING CORP.

PINNACLE BOOKS

are published by

Windsor Publishing Corp.
475 Park Avenue South
New York, NY 10016

Second printing: June, 1990

Printed in the United States of America

For a very real Ruby

VOODOO DIE

CHAPTER ONE

Nothing in Rev. Prescott Plumber's past prepared him for making death so easy for anyone who wanted to die, and if someone had told Plumber he would devise a prized war weapon, he would have smiled benevolently.

"Me? War? I am against war. I am against suffering. That is why I became a medical doctor, to use my skills for God and mankind." That is what he would have told people if he had not ended his life as a puddle on a palace floor.

When he left for the small jungle and volcanic rock island of Baqia, south of Cuba and north of Aruba, just off the sea lanes where British pirates had robbed Spanish treasure ships and called it war, the Rev. Dr. Plumber explained to another graduating student at medical school that serving God and mankind was the only worthwhile medical practice.

"Bulldooky," said his classmate in disgust. "Derma-

1

tology, and I'll tell you why. Unlike surgery, your insurance premiums aren't out of sight. And nobody ever woke a dermatologist up at four A.M. for an emergency acne operation. Your nights are your own, your days are your own, and anybody who thinks they ought to have a face as smooth as surgical rubber is always good pickings."

"I want to go where there is suffering, where there is pain and disease," said Plumber.

"That's sick," said the classmate. "You need a psychiatrist. Look, dermatology. Take my advice. The money's in skin, not God."

At the Baqian National Airport, Rev. Plumber was met by the mission staff in an old Ford station wagon. He was the only one who perspired. He was taken to the offices of the Ministry of Health. He waited in a room, whose walls were covered with impressive charts about ending infant mortality, upgrading nutrition, and providing effective home care. When he looked closer, he saw the charts were bilingual advertisements for the city of Austin, Texas, with Baqia stickers pasted over Austin's name.

The minister for health had one important question for this new doctor serving the mission in the hills:

"You got uppers, señor?"

"What?" asked Dr. Plumber, shocked.

"Reds. You got reds? You got greens? I'll take greenies."

"Those are narcotics."

"I need them for my health. And if I don't get them for my health, back you go to the States, gringo. You hear? Eh? Now, what you prescribe for my bad nights, Doctor, greens or reds? And my bad mornings, too."

2

"I guess you could call them greens and reds," said Dr. Plumber.

"Good. A pickup truck of reds and a pickup truck of greens."

"But that's dealing in drugs."

"We poor emerging nation. Now what you do here, eh?"

"I want to save babies."

"Dollar a kid, señor."

"Pay you a dollar for every child I save?" Dr. Plumber shook his head as if to make sure he was hearing right.

"This our country. These our ways. You laugh at our culture, señor?"

The Rev. Dr. Prescott Plumber certainly didn't want to do that. He came to save souls and lives.

"You get the souls free and because I like señor and because you are my brother from way up north, and because we are all part of the great American family we let you save the babies for twenty-five cents apiece, five for a dollar. Now where else you get a deal like that? Nowhere, yes?"

Dr. Plumber smiled.

The mission was in the hills that ringed the northern half of the island. The mission hospital was cinderblock and tin roofed with its own generator for electricity. Only one Baqian city had electricity and that was the capital, Ciudad Natividado, named for the Nativity of Christ by a Spanish nobleman, in gratitude for five successful years of rape and pillage between 1681 and 1686.

When he had first arrived at the mission, Dr. Plumber was amused to hear drums thumping in the distance. He decided it was probably the natives' signal system to alert everyone that a new doctor had ar-

3

rived. But the drums never stopped. From morning till night, they sounded out, forty beats a minute, never stopping, never varying, steadily insinuating their sound into Dr. Plumber's brain.

He was there alone for a week, without a patient, without a visitor, when one high noon the drums stopped. They had already become such a part of his life that, for a moment, Dr. Plumber did not realize what had happened, what strange new factor had intruded itself into his environment. And then he realized what it was. Silence.

Dr. Plumber heard another unusual sound. The sound of feet. He looked up from his seat at an outdoor table where he had been going over the mission's medical records. An old man with black trousers, no shirt, and a top hat, was approaching him. The man was small and hard-looking, with skin the color of a chestnut.

Plumber jumped to his feet and extended his hand. "Nice to see you. What can I do for you?"

"Nothing," the old man said. "But I can do for you. I am called Samedi." He was, he explained, the *hungan*, the holy man of the hills, and he had come to see Dr. Plumber before he would allow his people to visit the mission hospital.

"All I want is to save their bodies and their souls," said Dr. Plumber.

"That is a very big all-I-want," the old man said with a faint smile. "You may have their bodies to treat, but their souls belong to me."

And because that was the only way he would ever get any patients, Dr. Plumber agreed. At least for the time being, he would not try to convert anybody to any religion.

"Fine," Samedi said. "They have a very good religion of their own. Your patients will begin to arrive tomorrow."

Without another word, the old man got up and walked away. As he left the mission compound, the drums began again.

The patients arrived the next day, first a trickle, then a flood, and Plumber threw himself into the work he knew God had meant him to do. He treated and he healed.

Soon he installed an operating room with his own hands. He was a bit of an electrician, too. He rebuilt an X-ray machine.

He saved the life of the minister of justice and was thereafter allowed to save babies for nothing, although the minister of justice pointed out that if he saved just two good-looking female babies, he could put them to work in fourteen or fifteen years at the good hotels, and if they didn't get diseased, they would be good for at least $200 a week apiece, which was a fortune.

"That's white slavery," said Dr. Plumber, shocked.

"No. Brown is the lighest color you get. You don't get white ones. Black ones, they don't make too much. If you get blonde white one by some accident, you made, yes? Send her to me. We make money, no?"

"Absolutely not. I have come here to save lives and to save souls, not to pander to lust."

And the look the Rev. Dr. Plumber got was the same as the one given him by the medical student who planned on dermatology. The look said he was crazy. But Dr. Plumber didn't mind. Didn't the Bible tell him he should be a fool for Christ, which meant that others would think him a fool, but they were those who had not been blessed with the vision of salvation.

The dermatologist was the fool. The minister for health had been the fool, for right here in the Lord's dark brown earth was a substance, called "mung" by the villagers, which when packed against the forehead relieved depression. How foolish it was, thought Dr. Plumber, to deal in narcotics when the earth itself gave so much.

For several years, as he rebuilt the mission clinic into a full-fledged hospital, Dr. Plumber thought about the earth called mung. He made experiments and determined to his satisfaction that the mung did not seep through skin and therefore it had to affect the brain by rays. A young assistant, Sister Beatrice—unmarried, like the doctor himself—arrived at the mission one day with the distinction of being the first white woman to pass through Ciudad Natividado without being propositioned. Her stringy brown hair, thick glasses and teeth, which looked as if they had collided beyond the ability of modern orthodontics to straighten them out, had more to do with her freedom from pesty men than her virtue.

Dr. Plumber fell instantly in love. All his life he had saved himself for the right woman and he realized that Sister Beatrice must have been sent to him by the Lord.

More cynical Baqians might have pointed out that Caucasians working among the natives for three months tended to fall in love with their own kind within five seconds. Two minutes was an all-time record of composure for a white working among Baqians.

"Sister Beatrice, do you feel what I feel?" asked Dr. Plumber, his long bony hands wet and cold, his heart beating with anxious joy.

"If you feel deeply depressed, yes," said Sister

Beatrice. She had been willing to suffer all manner of discomfort for Jesus, but somehow suffering discomfort seemed more religious while friends and relatives were singing hymns in the Chillicothe First Church of Christianity. Here in Baqia, the drum sounds twenty-four hours a day pounded at her temples like hammer thuds, and cockroaches were cockroaches, and not a bit of grace about them.

"Depression, my dear?" said Dr. Plumber. "The Lord has provided from his earth."

And in a small laboratory he had built with his own hands, Dr. Plumber pressed the greenish black mung to Sister Beatrice's forehead and temples.

"That is wonderful," said Sister Beatrice. She blinked and blinked again. She had taken tranquilizers at times in her life and to a degree they had always made her drowsy. This substance just snapped you out of it, like a rubber band. It didn't make you overly happy, to be followed by a trough of unhappiness. It didn't make you excited and edgy. It just made you undepressed.

"This is wonderful. You must share this," said Sister Beatrice.

"Can't. Drug companies were interested for a while, but a handful of mung lasts forever and there's no way they can put it in expensive pills for people to take over and over again. As a matter of fact, I believe they might kill anyone trying to bring it into the country. It would ruin their tranquilizer and antidepressant market. Put thousands out of work. The way they explained it, I'd be robbing people of jobs."

"What about medical journals? They could get word to the world."

"I haven't done enough experiments."

"We'll do them now," said Sister Beatrice, her eyes

7

lit like furnaces in a winter storm. She saw herself as assistant to the great missionary scientist, the Rev. Dr. Prescott Plumber, discoverer of depression relief. She saw herself appearing at church halls, telling about the heat and the drums and the cockroaches and the filth of missionary work.

That would be so much nicer than working in Baqia, which was the pits.

Dr. Plumber blushed. There was an experiment he had been planning. It had to do with rays.

"If we shoot electrons through the mung, which I believe is actually a glycolpolyaminosilicilate, we should be able to demonstrate its effect on cell structure."

"Wonderful," said Sister Beatrice, who had not understood one word he had said.

She insisted he use her. She insisted he do it now. She insisted that he use full force. She sat down in a wicker chair.

Dr. Plumber put the mung in a box over a heavy little gas generator that provided electricity for the tubes that emitted electrons, smiled at Sister Beatrice, and then fried her to a gloppy stain seeping through the wicker.

"Oh," said Dr. Plumber.

The stain was burnt umber and the consistency of molasses. It seeped through what had been a plain white blouse with a denim skirt. The thick-soled plastic shoes were filled up to the top with the slop.

It smelled like pork fried rice left out in the tropical sun for a day. Dr. Plumber lifted the edge of the blouse with a tweezer. He saw she had worn a little opal on a chain. That was untouched. The bra and snaps were untouched. A cellophane bag that had held peanuts in her shirt pocket was safe, but the peanuts were gone.

Quite obviously, shooting electrons through the substance destroyed living matter. It probably rearranged the cell structure.

Dr. Plumber, a man who had found his one true love only to lose her immediately, made his way in a daze to the capital city of Ciudad Natividado.

He turned himself into the minister of justice.

"I have just committed murder," he said.

The minister of justice, whose life Dr. Plumber had saved, embraced the weeping missionary.

"Never," he screamed. "My friends never commit murder, not while I am minister of justice. Who was the communist guerilla you saved your mission from?"

"A member of my church."

"While she was strangling a poor native, yes?"

"No," said Dr. Plumber sadly. "While she was sitting innocently, helping me with an experiment. I didn't expect it to kill her."

"Better yet, an accident," said the minister of justice, laughing. "She was killed in an accident, yes?" He slapped Dr. Plumber on the back. "I tell you, gringo. Never let it be said of me that one of my friends ever went to jail for murder while I was minister of justice."

And thus it began. El Presidente himself found out about this wonderful thing you could do with mung.

"Better than bullets," said his minister of justice.

Sacristo Juarez Banista Sanchez y Corazon listened intently. He was a big man with dark jowls and a flaring black handlebar mustache, deep black eyes, thick lips, and a flat nose. Only in the last five years had he admitted to having black blood and then he did it with glory, offering his city to the Organization of Af-

9

rican Unity, saying, "Brothers should meet among brothers." Before that, he had explained to all white visitors that he was "Indian—no nigger in this man."

"Nothing better than bullets," said Corazon. He sucked a guava pit from a cavity in his front tooth. He would have to appear again at the United Nations, representing his country. He always did that when he needed dental work. Anything else could be left to the spirits, but major cavities could only be trusted to a man named Schwartz on the Grand Concourse in the Bronx. When Dr. Schwartz found out that Sacristo Juarez Banista Sanchez y Corazon was *the* Generalissimo Corazon, Butcher of the Caribbean, Papa Corazon, Mad Dog Dictator of Baqia, and one of the most bloodthirsty rulers the world had ever known, he did the only thing a Bronx dentist could. He tripled his prices and made Corazon pay in advance.

"Better than bullets," the minister of justice insisted. "Zap, and you got nothing."

"I don't need nothing. I need the dead bodies. How you going to hang a dead body in a village to show they should all love Papa Corazon, with all their minds and hearts, if you don't have no dead body? How you do this thing? How you run a country without bodies? Nothing better than bullets. Bullets are sacred."

Corazon kissed his thick fingertips, then opened his hands like a blossom. He loved bullets. He had shot his first man when he was nine. The man was tied to a post, his wrists bound with white sheets. The man saw the little nine-year-old boy with the big .45-caliber pistol and smiled. Little Sacristo shot the smile off the man's face.

An American from a fruit company came one day

10

to Sacristo's father and said he should no longer be a bandit. He brought a fancy uniform. He brought a box of papers. Sacristo's father became El Presidente and the box of papers became the constitution, the original of which was still in the New York office of the public relations agency that wrote it.

The American fruit company grew bananas for a while, and hoped to expand into mangoes. The mangoes didn't catch on in America and the fruit company pulled out.

Whenever anyone asked about human rights after that, Sacristo's father would point to that box over there. "We got every right you can think of and then some. We got the best rights in the world, yes?"

Sacristo's father would tell people that if they didn't believe him, they could open the box. Everyone believed Sacristo's father.

One day Sacristo's father heard that someone was planning to assassinate him. Sacristo knew where the assassin lived. Sacristo and his father went to slay the man. They took Sacristo's personal bodyguard of fifty men. Sacristo and the fifty men returned with his father's body. The father had fallen, bravely charging the enemy. He was killed instantly when he led the charge. No one thought it strange that he was killed by a bullet in the back of the head when the enemy was in front of him. Or if anyone thought it strange he did not mention it to Sacristo, who had been following his father, and was now El Presidente.

For allowing a potential enemy to kill his father, Sacristo personally shot the generals who were still loyal to his father.

Sacristo loved the bullet. It had given him everything in his life.

11

So El Presidente was not about to listen to tales that there were things better than bullets.

"I swear to you on my life it is better than bullets," said the minister of justice.

And Sacristo Corazon gave his minister a broad fat smile.

"As a figure of speech," said the minister, suddenly panicked by having wagered his life.

"Of course," said Corazon. His voice was soft. He liked the very big house of the minister of justice, and while it looked shabby on the outside there were marble floors and baths on the inside, and pretty girls who had never left the minister's compound.

And they were not even his own daughters. It was a fact of life that any family with a pretty daughter let her be deflowered by El Presidente or one of his cronies, or kept her forever behind closed doors. Now Corazon was a reasonable man. If a man prized his daughters, he could understand that man hiding them. But not the daughters of other men. That was sinful. To keep a girl from your leader, from El Presidente, was immoral.

So the minister of justice brought this thing that was supposed to be better than bullets. A missionary from the hill hospital came with a very heavy box. It was a two-foot cube and required great effort to move it.

The missionary was a doctor and a preacher and had been in Baqia several years. Corazon gave him the usual flowery praise due a messenger of God, then told him to perform his magic.

"Not magic, El Presidente. Science."

"Yes, yes. Go ahead. Who you going to use it on?"

"It's a health device and it failed. It failed to help

12

and it . . ." Dr. Plumber's voice crackled and faltered with his great sorrow. "It killed and it did not cure."

"Nothing more important than health. When you have health, you have everything. Everything. But let us see how it does not work. Let us see how it kills. Let us see if it is better than this," said El Presidente, and drew a shiny .44-caliber chrome pistol with mother-of-pearl handles, inlaid with the seal of the presidency and a good luck charm that, according to some of the voodoo priests, helped make the bullets go straighter, bullets having a mind of their own and at times defying the will of El Presidente.

Corazon pointed the shiny big-barreled pistol at the head of his minister of justice. "There are some who believe your box there better than bullets. There are some who bet their lives on it, no?"

The minister of justice had never realized how big, how truly big the barrel of a .44 was. It loomed like a dark tunnel. He imagined what a bullet might look like coming from it. If there were time to see. He imagined there would be a little explosion down at the other end of the barrel and then, *thwack*, he would not be thinking anymore because .44s tended to take out very big pieces of the brain, especially when the slugs were of soft lead with little dumdum holes in the center. There was a bullet waiting at the other end of that barrel.

The minister of justice smiled weakly. There was another element here, too. There were Western ways and island ways. The island ways were rooted in the hill religion known to the outside world as voodoo. Anyone bringing in the Western magic of science was pitting it against the island magic of voodoo.

Western magic was the plane. When the plane crashed, that was island magic. The island had won.

13

When the plane landed safely, it had won, especially when it landed safely with gifts for El Presidente.

So what was pitted now between the old reliable pistol and the machine of the missionary doctor was island magic in Corazon's hands and gringo industrialized magic in the hands of the bony, sad Dr. Plumber.

A pig was brought into the presidential chamber, a huge, domed, marble-floored formal room for giving medals, receiving ambassadors, and sometimes, when El Presidente had drunk too much, sleeping one off. He could lock the thick ironclad doors here and not be murdered in a drunken sleep.

The pig was a sow and reeked of recent mud, which was dried gray on her massive sides. Two men had to poke her with large sharp sticks to keep her from trampling everything in sight.

"There. Do it," said Corazon suspiciously.

"Do it," said the minister desperately.

"You want me to kill the pig?"

"It have no soul. Go ahead," said Corazon.

"I've only done it once," said Dr. Plumber.

"Once, many times, always. Do it. Do it. Do it," said the minister of justice. He was crying now.

Dr. Plumber turned the switch on the battery that started the ignition on the small generator. Three quarters of the device was devoted to producing electricity which, in a civilized country, could be gotten with a wire cord and a plug and a socket. But here in Baqia, everything had to be overcome. Dr. Plumber felt very sad and while it was only two days since the awful accident with Sister Beatrice, she became more beautiful with each passing minute. His mind had even achieved what breast cream, exercise, and suc-

14

tion cups had failed at: He imagined her with a bosom.

Dr. Plumber checked the mung supply. He checked the level of power. He pointed a small lenslike opening in the front of the box at the pig and then released the electrons.

There was a zap like a tight piece of cellophane snapping and then a smell of roasting rubber and the 350-pound pig smoked briefly, crackled once, and settled into a greenish black glop that spread across the marble floor.

Not even the hide was left. The wooden poles that had been poking the pig were cinders, but the metal points were there. They had hit the floor as soon as the pig melted. And the goo rolled over them.

"Amigo. My blood friend. My holy man friend. I really like Christ," said Corazon. "He one of the best gods there ever was. He my favorite god from now on. How you do that?"

Dr. Prescott Plumber explained how the machine worked.

Corazon shook his head. "Which button you push?" he asked.

"Oh, that," said Dr. Plumber and showed Corazon the red button that started the generator and then the green one that released the electrons.

And then a horrible accident ensued. Corazon accidentally killed his minister of justice just as Plumber had accidentally killed beautiful Sister Beatrice. The room smelled like a smoldering garbage dump.

There were goose bumps on Dr. Plumber's skin. The rays created vibrations in people standing too near a target.

"Oh, God. This is awful," sobbed Dr. Plumber. "This is horrible."

15

"Sorry," said Corazon. And he said "Sorry" again when he accidentally put away a captain of the guard whom he suspected of blackmailing an ambassador from another country and not giving his president a cut. This was at the palace gate.

"Sorry," said Corazon and the driver of a car disappeared from the window of a sedan and the car went crazily off the dusty main road of Ciudad Natividado and into the veranda of a small hotel.

"I believe you did that on purpose," sputtered Dr. Plumber.

"Scientific exploration has its price, yes?" said Corazon.

By now his guards were hiding, no one was in a window, and everywhere Corazon lugged the heavy thing, people hid. Except for tourists in the Hotel Astarse across the street. They watched, wondering what was going on, and Corazon did not zap them. He was no fool. He was not going to frighten away the Yankee dollar.

And then his luck changed. He found a soldier sleeping on duty in the palace.

"Punishment is needed," Corazon said. "I will have discipline in my army."

But by now Dr. Plumber was sure the machine had fallen into the hands of someone who killed on purpose. He put himself in front of the snoring Baqian corporal, who was sprawled in the island dust like a dozing basset hound.

"Over my dead body," said Dr. Plumber, defiantly.

"Okey-dokey," said Corazon.

"Okey-dokey what?" demanded Dr. Prescott Plumber, American citizen and missionary.

"Okey-dokey over your dead body," said Corazon, and with a bit of English—for with his natural talent

16

Corazon had found the rays took English somewhat like a billiard ball—he threw a little curve into the bony Dr. Plumber. A gold-covered bible suddenly appeared, resting on the metal part of a zipper, all atop a dark smelly puddle where Dr. Plumber had stood.

The Bible sank into the slop, pushing the strand of zipper beneath it. There were little bumps at the edges. Dr. Plumber had worn old-style shoes with nails in the heel. The nails remained.

When word reached the American State Department that one of its citizens had been coldly murdered just for the fun of it by the Mad Dog of the Caribbean, Generalissimo Sacristo Corazon, and that Corazon had in his sole possession a deadly weapon he alone understood, the decision was clear:

"How do we get him on our side?"

"He *is* on our side," explained someone from the Caribbean desk. "We've been putting about two million a year into his pocket."

"That was before he could turn people into silly putty," said a military analyst.

He was right.

Generalissimo Sacristo Juarez Banista Sanchez y Corazon called a special third world resource conference at Ciudad Natividado and, in unison, 111 technological ambassadors voted that Baqia had "an inalienable right to glycolpolyaminosilicilate" or, as the chairman of the conference said, "that long word on page three."

The world response was eight books on how Corazon had been slandered by the industrialized world's propaganda, a resurgence of interest in the deep philosophical meaning of the island's voodoo religion, and an international credit line for Corazon of up to three billion dollars.

The ships were stacked up outside Natividado harbor for miles.

In Washington, the President of the United States called the top representatives of his intelligence, diplomatic, and military establishments together and asked, "How did that lunatic down there get hold of something so destructive and what are we going to do to get it out of his hands?"

To this call for help, the answer was generally contained in long memos, each declaring, "You can't blame this department."

"All right," said the President, opening another meeting on the subject. "What can we do about this maniac down there? What is that weapon he's got? Now I want to hear suggestions. I don't care whose fault it is."

The gist of the meeting was that each department didn't have to handle it because it wasn't their responsibility, and no, they didn't know how the gizmo worked.

"There are only two things you people know. One, you're not guilty and two, don't ask you to do anything lest you become guilty of something. Have all these Congressional hearings made you into cowards?"

Everybody looked at the CIA director, who cleared his throat for a long time before replying. "Well, Mister President, if you don't mind my saying so, the last time somebody in my job tried to protect America's interests like that, your Justice Department tried to send him to jail. It doesn't exactly inspire us all with extracurricular zeal. No Congressional hearing ever blamed anybody for what he didn't do. None of us wants to go to jail."

"Isn't there anyone who cares that an American citizen has been killed? In all the reports, that was the least important thing," said the President. "Is there no one who is worried that a mad dog killer is on the loose with a dangerous weapon we have no defense against because we don't know how it works? Doesn't anyone care? Will someone speak up?"

Generals and admirals cleared their throats. Men responsible for the nation's foreign policy looked away, as did the chiefs of intelligence.

"To hell with you all," said the President in a soft Southern drawl. His face flushed red. He was as angry at the defense establishment as he was at himself for swearing.

If there wasn't any legal organization that could take care of this mess, then there certainly was an illegal one.

Midday, he retired to the Presidential bedroom in the White House and, reaching into a bureau drawer, put his hand on a red telephone without dials. He hated this phone and hated what it represented. Its very existence said his country could not operate within its own laws.

He had thought of abolishing the organization to which this one telephone was attached and which operated in emergencies, doing things he didn't want to know about. He thought at first he could quietly put the organization to rest. But he found he could not.

In a pinch, there was only one group he could count on and he sadly realized that it was illegal. It represented everything he hated.

It had been created more than a decade earlier, when covert operations were standard. And so deadly and so secret had been this organization, called CURE, that it alone, of all America's intelligence network, had escaped public inquiry without ever coming to light.

The CIA and military alike were open books, while no one but the President knew of CURE.

And, of course, its director and two assassins. The government, his government, supported two of the deadliest killers who ever existed in all the history of mankind and all he had to do was say to the director of CURE: "Stop."

And the organization would cease to exist. And the assassins would not work in America anymore.

But the President had never said stop, and it bothered his righteous soul to its deepest roots.

Even worse, he was about to find out that day that now he no longer had that illegal arm.

CHAPTER TWO

His name was Remo and the lights went out all around him. To most people in New York City, it was light, then suddenly blackness, in the summer night. The air conditioners stopped, the traffic lights disappeared, and suddenly people out on the street noticed the dark sky.

"What?" said a voice from a stoop.

"It's the 'lectricity." And then frightened noises. Someone laughed very loud.

The laughter did not come from Remo. He had not been plunged into sudden darkness. The lights did not go out for him in a split second.

For him there had been a flutter of light and then it died, in the street bulb above 99th Street and Broadway. It was a slow giving up, quite obvious if your mind and body rhythms were attuned to the world around you. It was only an illusion that there was sudden blackness. People helped this illusion, Remo knew.

They were engrossed in conversation, tuning out other senses to concentrate on their words, and they only tuned back the senses when they were already in darkness. Or they were drinking alcohol, or had loaded their stomachs with so much red meat that their nervous systems devoted all energies to laboriously processing it in an intestine designed for fruits and grains and nuts, and in a bloodstream that had ancient memories of the sea and could absorb quite well those special nutrients that came from fish. But never hoofed meat.

So it was dark and he had seen it coming and someone shrieked because she was afraid. And someone else shrieked because she was happy.

A car came up the block and lit it with its headlights and there was a noise in the streets of the city people, a mingling of nervous voices trying to establish contact in what they thought was a suddenly unnatural world.

And only one man in the entire city understood what was happening, because he alone had reawakened to his senses.

He knew that young men were running up behind him. It was not strange to listen for that or to know where their hands were and that one had a lead object he was trying to crack down on Remo or that the other had a blade. They moved their bodies that way.

You could explain it in a few hours to someone, using motion pictures of how every person gave obvious signs of their weapons by the way they moved their bodies. Some you could even tell what sort of weapon they had by looking at their feet alone. But the best way was feel.

How did Remo know? He knew it. Like he knew his head was on his shoulders and that the ground was down. Like he knew he could slow-catch the force of the lead object and readjust the boy's momentum to send him down into the concrete sidewalk so that he cracked his own ribs on collision.

The blade was simpler. Remo decided to use force.

"You're going to kill yourself with your own knife," Remo said softly. "Here we go."

He clasped the young man's hand around the knife so it could not let go and pressed it into the stomach, and feeling the blade had a sharpness to it he very slowly brought it up to where he felt the heart muscle throb against it.

"Oh, God," said the young man who knew now he was going to die and had not expected anything like that. He had done hundreds of stickings in New York City and no one had ever given him trouble, especially not when he worked with someone who used lead.

Sure, he had been arrested twice, once for cutting up a young girl who wouldn't give him any, but then he only spent a night in youth detention and he went back and settled with her.

He got her in an alley and he cut her up good. So good that they had to bury her in a closed coffin and her mother wept, and asked where justice was, and pointed a finger at him, but that was all she could do.

What was she going to do? Go to the police? He'd cut her up worse then. And what would they do? Give him a lecture? Put him up for a night in jail?

There was nothing that was going to happen to you for sticking someone in New York City. So it came as a great surprise to this young man that there would be some sort of violent objection from this person about to be mugged.

After all, he wasn't wearing a gang jacket, or riding around like he was connected to the mob, or wearing a gun. He had looked like a simple citizen of New York City, the kind anybody could do anything to. So what was this great pain he felt in his body? Was the guy a cop? There was a law against killing cops, but this guy didn't look like a cop.

They had been watching him just before the lights went. They had seen him buy a single flower from someone on Broadway and give the old woman a ten-dollar bill and tell her to keep the change.

And he had bills in his pocket. Then the guy took the flower, smelled it, and tore off two petals. And he chewed the damned things.

He was about six feet tall but skinny, and he had high cheekbones, as if he might have been part Chink or something. That's what one of the guys said. He had real thick wrists and he walked funny, like a shuffle. He looked easy. And he had money.

And when he turned into 99th Street, where it was not as well-lit and where no other citizens would come to his aid, where he was just beautiful pickings, the lights went out. Beautiful.

He didn't even wait. He knew he had a partner with a lead pipe, because that's what his partner was ready to use while the lights were on.

They closed in on the guy at the same time. It was beautiful, double beautiful. Wham. He should have collapsed.

But he didn't.

He hardly moved. You could feel him not move. You could make out that your partner fell onto the sidewalk like he was dropped off a roof. And then the guy spoke to you very softly and he had your hand in his and you couldn't even let go of the knife. And he punctured your belly and you slammed desperately at your own hand trying to get the knife out of it so it wouldn't tear your insides out, but it felt like someone had taped your belly button to the heating coil of an electric stove and that burn kept going up and you couldn't let go.

If you could have, you would have bitten your hand off at the wrist just to let go.

It hurt that bad.

When the heart went, when the muscle was pierced and his blood flowed out of his stomach and now very fast out, all over the place, and he finally was able to let go of the knife because the guy was walking on up the street, then it dawned on the young man, in the final clarity of the last moment of life, even a seventeen-year-old life, that this guy he had planned to stick had snuffed out his life without missing one slow shuffling step.

The young man's whole life was not even a missed step in the evening of that strange guy who ate the flower.

The city was dark and Remo moved on. There was some blood on his left thumb and he flicked it off.

The problem with people in the city, he knew, was that darkness, relying on your senses instead of mechanical means to produce artificial daylight, was the natural way. And suddenly people who did not even breathe properly found themselves having to use muscles they had never used before, atrophied muscles like those used to hear and see and feel.

He himself had been trained with great pain and great wisdom to learn how to revive the dormant skills of man, the talents that had once made man

25

competitive with the wild animals but now had turned this new species into walking corpses. The spear itself had made the human animal dependent on an outside thing, and not until the dawn of history in a fishing village on the west Korea bay did any man regain the pace and skill that reawakened what man could be.

The skill was called Sinanju, after the village in which it was created.

Only the Masters of Sinanju knew these techniques.

Only one white man had ever been so honored.

And that man was Remo and now in one of the great cities of his civilization the lights went out. And he was troubled.

Not because people were as people had been since before Babylon, but because he was now different.

And what had he done with his life? When he had agreed to undergo training, to serve an organization that would enable his country to survive, he thought there was a thing—justice—that he was working for.

And that changed as he became more like the Master of Sinanju who trained him. For then the perfection of being part of the House of Sinanju, the greatest assassins in all history, was enough. The doing of what you did was its very purpose. And one morning he awoke and he didn't believe that at all.

There was a right and there was a wrong and what was Remo doing that was right?

Nothing, he told himself. He moved on up to Harlem, walking slowly and thinking. Mobs had begun to loot and burn, and he came to the edge of one delirious crowd and saw it straining at an iron fence that shielded windows.

The sign behind the windows read: "Down Home Frozen Ribs."

It was obviously a black manufacturing plant. Not a big one either.

"Get 'im. Get 'im," yelled a woman and she was not yelling at Remo. Something up in front of the crowd was struggling against the mob, trying to keep it from breaking through the fence.

"Get the uppity nigger. Get the high-pants nigger. Get the uppity nigger," the woman yelled again. She had a quart bottle of gin in one hand and a baseball bat in the other.

If the crowd had not been black, Remo would have sworn it was made up of the Ku Klux Klan. Remo did not understand the hate. But he knew someone was struggling for what he had built. And that was worth protecting.

Remo moved, edging through bodies like a bowling ball through pins, glancing his own force against the stationary mass of those in front. The movement itself was like an unbroken, uninterrupted run and there was a shotgun pointing at his belly, and the man in front of the iron gate was black, and his finger was squeezing on the trigger as Remo flipped up the barrel and the blast went off above his head.

The mob hushed for a moment. Someone up front tried to run away. But when they saw the shot had been fired harmlessly and that the man wasn't going to kill, they charged again.

But the black man turned the barrel around and using the stock of the gun like the end of a club swung at Remo and then the crowd.

Remo avoided the wild slow arch of the gun butt, then worked the edge of the crowd toward the middle, until the man realized Remo was on his side. Then Remo took the center. In a few moments, he had a small barrier made of groaning people in front of the fenced factory front.

The crowd stopped pressing forward. They called to others passing by to get the white man they had trapped there. But there was too much fun out in the streets, where the only credit card you needed was a hammer and friends to help you tear away any protection in front of anything. Besides, this white man had a way of hurting people, so they turned and ran.

Remo stayed the night with the man, who had come from Jackson, Mississippi, as a little boy, whose father had worked as a janitor in a large office. The man had gotten a job in the post office and his wife worked and his two sons worked and they had all put their money into this small meat plant. Remo and the man stood out front and watched other shops go.

"Ah guess that's why I stayed here out 'n front wif a gun," the man said. "Mah sons are off buyin' direck from some farms in Jersey and ah didn't wan' to face them sayin' everything is gone. Death'd be easier than seein' this here go. It's our lives. That why I stayed. Why did you help?"

"Because I'm lucky," Remo said.

"Ah don' unnerstand."

"This is a good thing. This is a very good thing I do here tonight. I haven't done a good thing in a long while. It feels good. I'm lucky."

"That's pretty dangerous do-goodin'," said the man. "Ah almost shot you and ah almost banged you upside the haid with my shotgun, and if ah didn't get you, them mobs would. They's dangerous."

"Nah," said Remo. "They're garbage." He waved at the running crowds, laughing and screaming, dropping looted dresses from overladen arms.

"Even garbage can kill. You can get smothered by

28

garbage. And you move slow, too. Ah never saw no one fight like that."

"No reason you should have," Remo said.

"What that fightin' called?"

"It's a long story," Remo said.

"It ain' like karate. And it ain' like tae kwan do. Mah sons taught me that, for when I alone in the factory. You somethin' like that, but it ain' the same."

"I know," Remo said. "It only looks slow but it's really faster, what I do."

"It like a dance, but you very still about it."

"That's a good description. It is a dance, in a way. Your partner is your target. It's like you will do whatever you have to do and your partner is dead from the beginning. He sort of asks you to kill him and helps you do it. It's the unity of things." Remo was delighted at his own explanation, but the man looked puzzled and Remo knew he could never tell him what Sinanju was.

How do you explain to the whole world that it was, from its very first breaths, breathing wrong and living wrong? How did you explain that there was another way to live? And how did you explain to someone that you had been living that way and after more than ten years of it, you had decided it wasn't enough? There was more to life than breathing right and moving right.

When the sun came up red and glinted on the broken glass in the streets, when the police finally decided the streets were safe enough to return to duty, Remo left the man and never told him his name.

Without electricity, New York City was dead. Shows did not open and the arteries of the city's work force, the subway system, was a corpse of stopped trains waiting for the current of life.

29

It was hot and it felt like New York City had gone away for the day. Even Central Park was empty. Remo dawdled by the pond and when he got back to the Plaza Hotel it was noon. But he did not enter. He was stopped outside by a voice.

"Where have you been?" came the high squeaky voice.

"Nowhere," said Remo.

"You are late."

"How can I be late? I never said when I'd be back at the hotel."

"Woe be to the fool that would depend on you," said Chiun, Master of Sinanju, folding his long fingernails contemptuously into his golden morning kimono. "Woe be unto the fool that has given you the wisdom of Sinanju and, in return for this supreme knowledge, gets white lip. Thank you, no thank you, for nothing."

"I was thinking, Little Father," said Remo.

"Why bother to explain to a fool?" said Chiun. His skin was parchment yellow and his wisps of white beard and tufts of thin white hair around the borders of his skull quivered with the anger that was in him.

The skin was wrinkled and the lips were tight. He avoided looking at Remo. One might think this was a frail thin old man, but if one should test it out too thoroughly upon this Master of Sinanju, he would do no more testing on anyone ever.

"Okay, if you're not interested," Remo said.

"I am interested. I am interested in how one can pour a lifetime into an ingrate who does not even say where he goes or what he does or why he does it. I am interested in why a venerable, disciplined, wise, kind leader of his community would squander the treasure of wisdom that is Sinanju on someone who blows about like a dried leaf."

30

"All right. I was out last night because I had to think. . . ."

"Quiet. We don't have time. We are to go on a plane to Washington. We are now free of our bonds and we can work for a real emperor. You have never known this. It is far better than Smith, who I never understood. An insane emperor is like a wound to his personal assassin. We have been working with wounds, Remo. Now we are off."

With a flutter of his long fingernails, Chiun waved at bellboys. Fourteen ornately lacquered trunks stood on the white steps of the Plaza, partially blocking one of the entrances. Remo wondered how Chiun had gotten the bellboys to carry the heavy trunks down fourteen flights of stairs. When he saw one burly porter wince in fear as he passed Chiun, carrying a trunk to a cab, Remo knew. Chiun had that wonderful way of convincing people to help a poor little old man. It was called a death threat.

Two cabs were needed to go to the airport.

"What's going on?" Remo asked. He knew that Chiun never quite understood the organization or Dr. Harold Smith, who ran it. To Chiun, it did not make sense to have an assassin and then keep it secret. He had told Remo, if you make known your ability to kill your enemies, you will find yourself with very few enemies. But Smith did not listen.

And even worse, Smith never used Remo and Chiun "effectively," according to Chiun. "Effectively" meant for Smith to ask Chiun to remove the current President so Smith could declare himself emperor. Or king.

And of course, at the same time he would proclaim the House of Sinanju official assassins to the nation and the Presidency. Chiun had it all worked out. He

31

had seen the recent American inauguration ceremony on television. Smith, who ran CURE and would under Chiun's plan run the country, would walk five paces ahead of Chiun in the parade and Chiun would wear his red kimono with the gold-threaded tana leaves. When Chiun told Smith how it would be, Smith said:

"Never."

"The green kimono, then, with the black swans."

"Never. Never."

"Gold is for mornings. Your inaugurations are afternoons," Chiun had explained reasonably.

"I will never assassinate our President. I don't want to be President. I serve the President. I serve the nation. I want to help him," Smith had said.

"We don't miss, like some of the amateurs walking around your streets," Chiun had replied. "You have nothing to fear. We can put you on your President's throne this very week. And our rates will be virtually the same. This is a big country with a turbulent, rebellious population. We might have to go a mite higher. But you would never miss it. Your cities alone are bigger than most countries."

"No," Smith had said. "I don't even want to discuss it."

Remo had interceded. "You're never going to convince Chiun that you are not a minor emperor who should be plotting against the big emperor, now that you have the House of Sinanju on your side. You're never going to convince him that there is only one form of government, with many different names like democracy and communism and monarchy. He thinks it's one man on top and most everyone else trying to take it away from him."

The conversation had all taken place two days ago in the waiting room of Newark Airport.

"And what do you think, Remo?" Smith asked.

"I think I am not going to Baqia."

"May I know why?" asked Smith. He was a gaunt, thin-lipped man and the years had not worn well on him. He was still in his middle age, but he already looked old.

"Yeah," said Remo. "I don't care what happens to the Caribbean. I don't care who kills who. All I know is that everything I've ever done for this outfit hasn't made two spits' difference in a rainstorm. We were supposed to make the Constitution work outside the Constitution, give it that extra little edge. Well, the country's become a garbage can and I don't see how one more corpse is going to help it, one way or another, and so it's no to Baqia. I don't care who is able to do what or which agency can't do what. No."

And Chiun had nodded affirmation to this. "However," added Chiun to Smith, "if you should change your mind about becoming emperor, I am sure Remo might be persuaded how good life can be working for a real emperor."

"I'm not going to Baqia," Remo said again.

"He'll go if you sit in the White House throne," said Chiun.

And that had been that. Smith had been shaken. Chiun had been angry because, as he said, Remo never understood the business aspects of assassinry and never listened when Chiun tried to explain, either.

Now, if Remo could believe what he was hearing in the cab on the way to LaGuardia Airport, Chiun had spoken personally to the President of the United States, who had invited him down for a visit.

"That's impossible," Remo said. "We work for an organization that doesn't exist. Its purpose is not to

33

exist. It's secret," Remo whispered harshly. "They are not proud in this country of employing assassins."

"Not until now. But nations grow," said Chiun.

"You mean we're supposed to walk right in the front door of the White House?" asked Remo.

"Not exactly," said Chiun.

"Aha. I thought so."

"But we will be received by the President himself."

"Ridiculous," said Remo. They had met the President once before, to show him how vulnerable the White House was to attack, that it was as open as a massage parlor to people who had made lifetime studies of walls and doors and windows. Remo had gone back to reinforce the lesson. The President hadn't listened and Chiun had met the President again when he was saving his life from a killer. Chiun had not waited for thanks.

That night, Chiun's bulky baggage checked at the Washington Hilton, they made their way into the White House and were in the oval office by 10:33 P.M., the time Chiun said the President had specified.

The two waited in the dark office.

"I feel stupid," Remo said. "We're going to sit here until morning and then scare the ditfrimmy out of some cleaning woman. Or whatever they use to straighten out an ultrasecure office."

"Ditfrimmy?" asked Chiun. "I have never heard of ditfrimmy."

"I made it up. It's a made-up word. I make up words sometimes."

"So do most babies," said Chiun with that calm feeling of having helped his student realize his proper place in relationship to the Master of Sinanju, who now waited in the American emperor's throne room, as Chiun's ancestors had waited in throne rooms for centuries, to assure pharaoh or king or emperor or President that this enemy or that would breathe his last, provided proper tribute was guaranteed to the little village of Sinanju on the west Korean bay.

The door opened. A crack of light was in the room. Someone just outside the door spoke.

"Guaranteed, Mr. President, sir. Impossible, sir, for anyone to get into your oval office, sir, without us finding out, sir. You're in a tight seal, if I may say so, sir."

"Thank you," answered the soft Southern voice.

And the President entered his office, shut the door behind himself, and personally turned on the lights.

"Hello," he said.

"Greetings to the heir of Washington and Lincoln and Roosevelt," intoned Chiun, rising, then bowing low. "Hail to the triumphant successor of Rutherford B. Hayes and Millard Fillmore. Of the redoubtable James K. Polk and Grover Cleveland. Of the beneficent James Madison and Calvin Coolidge the Great."

"Thank you," said the President with a small embarrassed smile. But Chiun was not finished.

"Of Ulysses Grant the Wise, of the handsome Andrew Johnson. Woodrow Wilson the Triumphant and Hoover the Magnificent. To say nothing of Andrew Jackson . . ."

"Thank you," said the President.

"Of William McKinley," said Chiun, who had read books about the new American land and like so many travelers found that the descriptions did not fit the people. "A happy robust people," had said the old Korean history of the world. It gave the United States a quarter of a page in a three-thousand-page volume, the first two-hundred-eighty pages of which were the

35

definitive work on the early dynasties of the Korean peninsula and their effect on the world.

"Of Grover Cleveland again," Chiun said with a delighted squeak.

"Thank you," said the President. Remo stayed slumped in his chair and wondered if the President kept anything in the drawers of the big polished desk in the oval office. The President offered his hand to Chiun. Chiun kissed it with a bow. He offered it to Remo. Remo looked at it as if a waiter had brought him creamed liver and scrod or some other untasty thing he had not ordered.

The President withdrew his hand. He sat on the edge of the desk with one leg raised along its edge, dangling from the knee. He examined his hands, then looked directly at Remo.

"We're in trouble," he said. "Are you an American?"

"Yes," said Remo.

"I heah you don't want to work for your country anymore. May I ask why?"

"Because he is an ingrate, O gracious President," said Chiun. "But we can cure him of that." And to Remo, in an angry tone but in Korean, Chiun warned that Remo should not mess up a good sale with his childish antics. Chiun knew how to handle this President. And one way was never let him know how little you thought of him.

Remo shrugged.

"Thank you," the President said to Chiun. "But I would like this man to answer."

"All right, I'll answer," Remo said. "You say work for the country. Bulldooky. I'm working so that this slop can stay afloat. Work for America? Last night I worked for America. I helped a man save his little factory. What did you do?"

"I did what I could. That's what I ask of you."

"Did you really? Why didn't the police protect victims last night? Why didn't you order them to? Why didn't anyone order them to?"

"The problems of poverty—"

"It wasn't a poverty problem. It was a police problem. There's right and wrong in the world and you people and people like you fudge up the whole damned thing with your sociology. Everyone knows right and wrong except you politicians." Remo looked away in anger.

Chiun assured the President that Remo's sudden outburst was nothing to worry about.

"As a student nears perfection, there is often a throwback to pretraining ideas. The Great Wang himself, when he was close to the height of his powers, would play with a toy wagon his father had made him, and this while in service to Cathay."

Chiun wondered if he could interest the President in something closer to home. Perhaps the kidnaping of his vice president's favorite child. This often assured an emperor that the one destined to take his throne in case of an accident would remain loyal.

"Ambition," said Chiun sadly, "is our greatest enemy. Let us cure the vice president of this woeful malady."

"That's not what I want," said the President. He did not take his eyes off Remo.

"A congressman," offered Chiun. "Perhaps a painful death at a public monument with a cry of 'death to all traitors, long live our divine President.' That is always a good one."

"No."

"A senator horribly mutilated while he sleeps and the word discreetly spread among other senators that

37

he was plotting treason." Chiun gave a big happy wink. "A most popular item, that one."

"Remo," said the President. "The Central Intelligence Agency is afraid to get its hands dirty anymore, assuming it could ever do what we need done. There is a madman on an island close to America and he's got something that fries people to the consistency of Crest toothpaste. The Russians are interested in it. So are the Chinese, the Cubans, the British, and God knows who else, but our people sit back here terrified of making a mistake. We are incapable of dealing with a menace close to home. Do you think I would have asked you here to beg you to take an assignment? We're in trouble. Not just me, not just the office, not just the government. Every man, woman, and child in this country and possibly the world is in trouble because somehow some killer got hold of one of the most frightening weapons I have ever heard of. I am asking you to get control of that weapon on behalf of the human race."

"No," said Remo.

"He doesn't mean that," said Chiun.

"I think he does," said the President.

"At one time, Greek fire was a strange and frightening weapons, O Imperial Glory of the American People. Yet, it died, and why?" asked Chiun.

"I don' know why," said the President. He stared at Remo, who did not lift his eyes to make contact.

"Because that Byzantine emperor, the last to control the formula for the fire that burns when you add water, insulted the House of Sinanju and his fire proved no menace to the hands of Sinanju. He died with his supposedly invincible weapon. If you want something done along that line, it would be simple."

"Done," said the President.

38

"You'll be sorry," said Remo.

"No sorrier than I am now," the President said.

"Would you like the Baqian tyrant's head for the White House gate?" asked Chiun. "It is a traditional finish to this sort of assignment. And, I might add, a most fitting one."

"No. We just want the weapon," the President said.

"A splendid selection," said Chiun.

CHAPTER THREE

When the Third World Conference on Material Resources left Baqia after a triumphal unanimous declaration that Baqia had an inalienable right to that big word on page three, Generalissimo Sacristo Corazon declared a general amnesty to all prisoners, in honor of Third World brotherhood.

The Baqian jail had forty cells but only three prisoners because of a very efficient system of justice. Criminals were either hung, sent to the mountains to work in the great tar pits, which provided 29 percent of the world's asphalt, or released with apologies.

The apologies came after a $4,000 contribution to the Ministry of Justice. For $10,000, one got "profuse" apologies. An American lawyer once asked Corazon why they didn't just declare a person innocent.

"That's what *we* do when we buy off a judge," the lawyer said.

"It lack class. For ten tousan', you got to give something," Corazon answered.

Now, in the hot dusty road leading from the main highway to the prison compound, set back in a dry powdery field that looked like a desert, Corazon waited with his black box at his side. It was on wheels now and had padlocks and a new profusion of dials. The dials were not attached to anything; Corazon had attached them himself in the darkest part of the night. If Generalissimo Corazon knew anything, it was how to survive as ruler of Baqia.

His new minister of justice and all his generals were there. It was a hot day. The new minister of justice waited outside the prison's high gates for the signal from Corazon to release the prisoners.

"Umibia votes yes," called out someone drunkenly. It was a delegate who had missed his plane back to Africa and joined the Corazon caravan, thinking it was a taxi to the airport.

"Get that fool out of the way," snapped Corazon.

"Umibia votes yes to that," called out the man. He wore a white, glistening suit, sprinkled with the refuse of two days of heavy drinking. He held a bottle of rum in his right hand and a gold chalice some fool had left in a little stone box in a Western religion church.

He poured the rum toward the gold chalice. Sometimes he made it into the bowl. Sometimes the rum added a new flavor to his suit. He wanted to drink his suit but the buttons kept getting in the way.

This was his first diplomatic assignment and he was celebrating its success. He had voted "yes" at least forty times more than anyone else. He expected a medal. He saw himself being honored at another conference as the finest delegate in the entire world.

And then he made his first serious mistake. He saw the big dark face of Generalissimo Corazon with all his medals gleaming in the noon sun. He saw his Third World brother. And he wanted to kiss him. He was also standing upwind of the Generalissimo. The Umibian delegate smelled like a saloon that hadn't opened its windows since Christmas.

"Who is that man?" asked Corazon.

"One of the delegates," answered the minister for foreign affairs and head chauffeur.

"Is he important?"

"His country doesn't have oil, if that's what you mean. And it has no foreign agents," whispered the minister.

Corazon nodded.

"Beloved defenders of Baqia," he boomed. "We have declared an amnesty in honor of our Third World brothers. We have shown mercy. But now there are those who confuse mercy with weakness."

"Bastardos," called out the generals.

"We are not weak."

"No, no, no," called out the generals.

"But some think we are weak," said Corazon.

"Death to all who think we are weak," shouted one general.

"I am a slave to your will, oh, my people," said Generalissimo Corazon.

He estimated the drunken weave of the Umibian ambassador. He knew everyone watched. And so he carefully began turning the dials he had attached the night before. Because if his government ever found out that all you had to do was point the machine and start the engine that did whatever it did, one might be tempted to jump the Generalissimo and become the new leader. Corazon understood a very simple

43

rule of governing. Fear and greed. Make them frightened enough and satisfied with their stealing enough and you had stable government. Let any one of those things get out of whack and you had trouble.

"One point seven," said Corazon loudly and turned the blue dial a bit. He saw two ministers and a general move their lips. They were repeating the number to themselves. It was the ones who could memorize without moving their lips that he had to fear.

"Three-sevenths," said Corazon and flicked a switch three times. He licked his right thumb and put the thumbprint on top of the box.

"My spit. My power. O powers of machine, the powerful one of this kingdom shares his power with you. Alight. Alight and recognize power. My power. Me big number one."

And very quickly he hit every dial with a turn or a flick, and just about midmaneuver he flipped the real switch that triggered the gas engine.

The engine purred and whatever was supposed to happen was happening.

There was a loud crack from the machine and then a cool greenish glow enveloped the delegate from Umibia. The man smiled.

Panicked, Corazon smacked all the buttons again. The machine crackled again. The glow again enveloped the Umibian diplomat. He smiled, teetered backwards, then regained his forward momentum towards Corazon. He wanted to kiss his Third World brother. He wanted to kiss the world.

Unfortunately, black gooey puddles just off Route 1 in Baqia had no lips and could not kiss. The bottle of rum fell into the dry dirt and spilled wetness into the dust, a small irregular circle similar to what was now left of the Umibian delegate. Even the buttons were gone.

44

The generals cheered. The ministers cheered and all pledged their lifelong fealty to Corazon. But the Generalissimo was worried. For some reason the machine had taken longer to work this time than it generally did. This the generals and ministers did not know, but Corazon did.

The minister of agriculture borrowed a riding crop from a general and poked around in the goo until he latched onto something. He lifted it up, borrowed a cup of water from a soldier with a machine gun in his lap, and cleaned off the goo. A new Seiko watch. He offered it first to the Generalissimo.

"No," said Corazon. "For you. I love my people. It is your watch. We are sharing. This is socialism. A new socialism." And he pointed to the jail door and said, "Open the gates."

And the minister of defense swung open the big jail doors, and three people came out into the roadway.

"By my beneficence and in the surety of my great power, you are all free in honor of the Third World Natural Resource Conference or whatever. I free you in honor of our having inalienable rights to everything."

"That one's a spy," whispered the minister of defense, pointing to a man in a blue blazer and white slacks and a straw hat. "British spy."

"I freed him already. Why you tell me now? Now we gotta find other reasons to hang him."

"Won't help," said the minister of defense. "We're crawling with them. Must be a hundred spies from all over the world and other places."

"I know that," said Corazon angrily. For on Baqia a man who did not know things showed weakness and the weak were dead.

45

"Do you know that they are killing themselves all over Ciudad Natividad? In our very capital?"

"I know that," said Corazon.

"Do you know, El Presidente, that our army has difficulty controlling the streets? Every nation has brought in its best killers and spies to get our precious resource," said the minister of defense, pointing to the black box with dials. "They have filled the Astarse Hotel. They want that."

"Who has the most here?"

"The Russians."

"Then we blame the Central Intelligence Agency for tampering with our internal affairs."

"They only got one man and he can't carry a gun even. They're afraid of their own people. The Americans are weak."

"We'll have a trial, too," Corazon said with a grin. "The best trial in the Caribbean. We'll have a hundred jurors and five judges. And when time comes for verdict, they will stand up and sing—'Guilty, guilty, guilty.' Then we hang the American spy."

"Can I have his watch?" asked the new minister of justice. "Agriculture just got one."

Corazon thought a moment. If the American spy was the middle-aged gentleman with the gray jeep who said he was a prospector, then that man had a gold Rolex. That was a very good watch.

"No," said Corazon. "His watch is the property of the state."

The trial was held on the afternoon the American was called into the presidential palace. One hundred jurors proved too unwieldy so they settled on five. Since Corazon had heard that in America juries were of mixed races, he had three Russians sit on the jury

46

because he realized, wisely, to a television camera white is white.

The verdict was guilty as charged and the man was hanged by noon. Corazon gave seashell wrist bracelets in thanks to all the jurors. The bracelets came from a novelty shop in the basement of the Astarse Hotel. Two of the jurors, both Russians, wanted to see how the Generalissimo's wonderful machine worked. They had heard so much about it and they would love to see it before those evil imperialist American capitalist CIA warmongering adventuring spies stole it.

Corazon laughed. Agreed. Promised he would. Sent them to the far side of the island and waited for his men to return to tell him that the Russians were disposed of. His men didn't return. Ooops, better be careful.

Corazon called in the Russian ambassador to talk out a special peace pact. Anyone who could survive on a strange island against Corazon's soldiers was to be respected. So Corazon talked of friendship treaties.

The news of the treaty between Baqia and Russia arrived in America at the same time as the news clip of the "American spy" being hanged.

A commentator for a major network who had a smothered Virginia drawl and a righteous but somewhat jowly face asked the question: "When is America going to stop failing with spies, when we can succeed so much better with moral leadership, a moral leadership that Russia cannot hope to offer?"

About the same time that this commentator, who was addicted to labeling happenings he didn't understand as good things or bad things, went off the air, a heavily-lacquered steamer trunk was dropped carelessly on the sticky asphalt runway of the Baqian International Airport and America's diplomatic prestige was about to spring back from the depths.

The trunk was one of fourteen, each with its original polished wood carefully painted. This one was green. The porter did not think that some old Oriental, especially one traveling under an American passport, was anything to concern himself about. Particularly since the porter had more important things to do, like tell the army captain standing under the wing about a second cousin's ability to crush a cocoanut with rum and make a drink that would leave you stupefied.

"You have dropped one of my trunks," said Chiun to the porter. The old man was a picture of repose. Remo carried a small tote bag, which had everything he would need for months: another pair of socks, a change of shorts, and another shirt. Any time he stayed more than one day in one spot, he bought everything else he needed. He wore gray summer chinos and a black T-shirt and didn't particularly like the Baqian International Airport very much. It looked like aluminum and grass dropped into a scrub swamp. A few palm trees dotted the sides of the airport. Far off were the mountains where it was said the greatest voodoo doctors in the world practiced medicine and, as Remo listened, he could hear the thump of the drums, sounding out over the island as if it were the Baqian heartbeat. Remo looked around and sniffed. Just another normal Caribbean dictatorship. To hell with it. This was Chiun's show and if the United States wanted Chiun to represent it, let them find out what a Master of Sinanju was like.

Remo did not know much about diplomacy but he was certain Ming dynasty terror would not be too effective here on Baqia. Then again, who knew? Remo

48

stuffed his hands into his pockets and watched Chiun deal with the Baqian captain and porter.

"My trunk has been dropped," said Chiun. The captain, who had a new gold-trimmed captain's hat and new black combat boots, shined so he could see his face in them, outweighed the old Oriental by one-hundred pounds, fifty of it hanging over his own black belt. He knew the Oriental was carrying an American passport, so he spat on the runway.

"I talking, Yankee. I don't like Yankee and I don't like yellow Yankee most of all."

"My trunk has been dropped," said Chiun.

"You talking Baqian captain. You show respect. You bow."

The Master of Sinanju folded his long fingers into his kimono. His voice was sweet.

"What a great tragedy," he said, "that there are not more people here to listen to your beautiful voice."

"What?" said the captain suspiciously.

"Let me punch that old gook in his face, yes?" asked the porter. The porter was twenty-two, with a fine young black face and the solid healthy gait of one who regularly exercised his body. He was 18 inches taller than Chiun and towered above the captain, also. He put two of his massive hands on either side of the green lacquered trunk and lifted it above his head. "I crush the yellow Yankee, yes?"

"Wait," said the captain, his hand on his bulging .45-caliber pistol on his belt. "What you mean, yellow man, that I sing nice?"

"Very nicely," said Chiun, his voice as sweet as a nightingale. "You will this day sing 'God Bless America' and mean it so profoundly that all will say your voice is as sweet as lark's whisper."

49

"I choke on me tongue first, yellow man," spat the captain.

"No," said Chiun. "You choke on your tongue later."

There was a bit of delicacy required in this. The green trunk held tapes of American daytime television dramas and they might not have been packed that solidly. They had to come down gently from above the porter's head, where he still held the trunk, so with a smooth and constant rhythm Chiun's hands flashed out and closed on the left knee of the porter and then the right. It looked as if the old parchment hands were warming the knees. The captain waited for the porter to drop the trunk and crush the fool.

But then the captain saw the porter's knees do what he had never before seen knees do. There were the shoes. There were the shins and the knees just seemed to sink inside the pants down into the shoes—and the porter was eighteen inches shorter. And then the waist seemed to collapse and the old Oriental in the kimono moved around the porter like a peeling machine and a look of horror was on the porter's face, his mouth opening to scream but the lungs were a mess just beneath his throat and the trunk teetered on the top of his head momentarily, but then his chin was on the runway and his hands were stretched out lifeless beneath it and, with one long fingernail, the Oriental was under the trunk, working the porter's head, until the green lacquer glittered above its blood and pulp base. The television tapes were safe.

The porter was not much more than a stain.

"God, He bless America," sang the captain, hoping the tune somewhat resembled the gringo song. He sure smiled big for his American friends.

"We all called Americans," laughed the captain.

"Those are not the word to that great nation's song

50

which has wisely chosen to employ the House of Sinanju. Remo will teach you the words. He knows American songs."

"I know some of them," Remo said.

"What are the words?" begged the captain.

"I dunno," said Remo. "Hum something."

The captain, who always loved the United States with all his heart—he had a sister in the States and she loved America almost as much as he—ordered his company to make sure not one ounce of harm came to any of the trunks. He would shoot the first man who dropped one of the trunks. Personally he would do the shooting.

A corporal from Hosania Province, famous for the locals' laziness, complained about some dead and sticky meat underneath the green trunk on the runway.

The captain shot him through the head as an object lesson to all the soldiers in his command how neighbors should love each other and no one loved America more than the captain. Especially yellow Americans.

Eighty-five Baqian soldiers marched from the airport to the Astarse Hotel singing "God, He love America" to a conga beat. The fourteen trunks went atop their heads like some fat snake with shiny square parts.

The procession passed the presidential palace and went into the front door of the Astarse.

"Best room in house," said the captain.

"I'm sorry, captain. But all the rooms are filled."

"Rooms, they never filled at the Astarse. We have tourist problem."

"They fill now, hey hey," said the clerk. "They got weapons upstairs you never see. They got 'em big." And the clerk spread his arms. "They got 'em small."

51

And the clerk closed two fingers together. "And they use 'em good. We lose three soldiers yesterday. Yes, we do."

"I work at airport," said the captain. "I hear trouble here, but I don't hear what kind."

"Sure. Them soldier fellas, they don't tell you, captain, so when there's an order to come here, dummy fellas like you, you come and get killed, fella. That's what you get, fella."

"The bastards," muttered the captain. He was thinking of his superior officers. They must have known. They were offering assignments to watch tourists at lower rates. A captain in the Baqian army, like other Spanish-speaking officers everywhere, no matter what their politics, engaged in rugged-individualism capitalism.

They believed so fiercely in the free market system they would put a banker to shame. It was an honored tradition, no worse in Baqia than anywhere else in the Caribbean. One paid for a commission in the army. That was an investment. As an officer, you used your rank to earn back the investment with a profit. Sometimes, if you were poor, you repaid with loyalty. You bought good assignments. An airport with its commerce was fairly good. But a tourist hotel with its prostitutes and illegal smuggling sales was a delight in the generals' eyes. The captain had known there was trouble because the price for a hotel assignment was going down.

He had thought it was worth the risk and was going to put in a bid for the job. But now this generous clerk had warned him. Generous? The captain had suspicious second thoughts.

"Why you tell me this?" asked the captain. He hoisted his belly up briefly, a notch above his gunbelt.

"I don't want to be here when everybody tries to settle who has what room."

The captain rubbed his chin. This problem. He looked back at the delicate Oriental with the wisps of white hair. The captain smiled very broadly. He was not about to forget the porter, who was now a form of tapioca on the main runway of the International Airport. Then again, if a clerk gave something for nothing, there must be something horrible upstairs.

"I give you free information," confided the captain. "It is in return for your free information. You better give that nice little old yellow man a room."

"I will, señor captain, right now. But first evict its occupants. You might want to start with the Bulgarians on the second floor. They have the machine gun covering the hallway and they put sandbags around the walls of their room, and this morning when I complained because they didn't send the bellboy back and they had no right to keep him upstairs that long, because we shorthanded down here, they send me this."

The clerk took a hatbox from beneath the counter and, turning his head, removed the cover. The captain peered in. Wrapped in wax paper were severed human hands.

"You look at remains of bellboy."

"He must have been a wonderful bellboy," commiserated the captain.

"Why you say that?" asked the clerk.

"How much help has three hands?"

The clerk peered into the box. "And the second cook, too. I didn't even know. And the Bulgarians are the peaceful ones."

The clerk went down a list. There were Russians and Chinese, British, Cubans, Brazilians, Syrians, Israelis, South Africans, Nigerians, and Swedes. There were also fourteen free-lance adventurers. All of them there to try to steal Baqia's new weapon.

"And I'm not counting the liberation groups still in the field waiting for rooms," said the clerk.

"Who's out now? Any of the rooms empty?" asked the captain.

"I'm afraid to check, but I think the British lobbed a couple of mortar shells down a stairwell early this morning. They usually do that when they go out for tea or something."

The captain clicked his heels and saluted.

"Señor American, we have a wonderful room for you," he said.

Crawling on their bellies, the first wave of Baqian enlisted men managed to get two trunks up the main stairway. One wedged open a door with a crowbar. The South Africans had opened up with small-arms fire that had been answered by the Russians, who thought the Bulgarians were at it again. Two Baqian corporals struggled back down the stairs, one clutching an arm shattered by a bullet that had left it dangling.

They had opened up a passage to move all the trunks into the second-floor east room and, except for a small booby trap at the door, there seemed to be no British presence in the room.

The clerk had been right. Second floor 2-E was temporarily unoccupied. All fourteen trunks managed to be winched and dragged into the room with only one more casualty. A young boy from the docks, who had just finished basic training a week before and whose father had paid to have him assigned to the airport, where he would have a chance for promotion without danger, caught a direct hit in the forehead.

54

He was brought down under a sheet that would have been white had it ever been washed.

When the way was cleared for the yellow American with the very unusual hands, Chiun entered 2-E. He stepped over the white sheet covering the young man just outside the entrance.

The captain waited nervously. He wanted to politely say goodbye to this dangerous American and also get out of the hotel with as many living men as possible.

"Where are you going?" asked Chiun.

"We have taken you to room, yes? You like, yes?"

"The towels are not clean. The sheets are not clean." Chiun looked toward the window. "Where is the bay? This room does not have a view of the bay. Those beds have been slept in. Where are the maids? Ice? There should be ice. I do not like ice, but there should be ice." Chiun examined the bathroom.

"The other rooms, they are no better, señor," said the captain.

"The ones that look over the bay are," said Chiun. "I bet they have clean towels and sheets too."

"Señor, we are greatly afraid, but someone of your illustrious wisdom and abilities and personage could succeed where we have failed. Should you arrange for another room, the Baqian armed forces stand ready to deliver your trunks. In salute to your magnificence."

Chiun smiled. Remo muttered under his breath that now he was going to hear how Chiun was finally getting the proper respect. Groveling servitude, like the captain's, always brought out the best in Chiun. Speech down, the captain backed out of the room. Chiun raised a single long fingernail toward Remo.

"As an assassin, you must learn not only to carry out your emperor's wishes, but to go beyond them to what not only is good but appears good. Your President thinks he wants a machine, quietly delivered, and the respect of the people of Baqia, and the world."

"Little Father," said Remo, "I think the President wants us in and out without trouble, *with* the doohickey that Corazon has. I think that's what he wants."

"There is a lack of elegance to that, you know," said Chiun. "It is like a thief, stealing."

"I was in the same oval office with the President that you were. I heard what he said."

Chiun smiled. "And if he wanted typical shoddy workmanship, he would have used American. He would have given the assignment to you. But no. He gave it to me. He has chosen Sinanju and thus his name, whatever it is, will shine in history."

"You don't know the name of the President of the United States?" asked Remo incredulously.

"You keep changing them," said Chiun. "I learned one. He had a funny name and then there was someone else. And soon there was someone else. And one of those was an amateur assassination." Chiun shook his head. He did not like America's penchant for amateur assassinations, hate killings, and all manner of devilment that made these people barbarians. What they needed and what they would now get was elegance, the sun source of all the martial arts, Sinanju.

Across the main street in the presidential palace compound, Dr. Bissel Hunting Jameson IV, second assistant director of the British Royal Academy of Science, did not know that his room had been taken by someone else.

He and his staff were all immaculately attired in

white summer trousers, blue blazer with Royal Academy seal, white bucks, school ties, and Walther P-38's tailored into their shirts. They held straw skimmers in their hands and they were the only ones ever seen in Baqia who could cross Route 1 in midday, midsummer, wearing these clothes without raising a sweat.

It was as if this race of men had been bred with internal cooling systems.

The offer being made by Dr. Jameson, in rich aristocratic English emanating from the bowels and resonating out through the mouth, with each vowel a trumpeting declaration of basic natural superiority, was this:

Britain shared Baqia's destiny. Britain too was an island. Britain, like Baqia, had national interests and faced currency problems. Together, Britain and Baqia could march forward exploiting both Baqia's new discovery and Britain's experience in manufacturing secret devices.

By the time Dr. Jameson finished, if one did not know that Baqia was an island slum of shacks and abandoned sugar fields and Britain was an industrialized nation somewhat on hard times, an observer would have concluded that Her Majesty's government and the current dictator of a rock protrusion in the Caribbean shared a common heritage and future.

Corazon listened to these white men.

They had paid what was now the standard fee to see the machine in operation. In gold. Corazon liked gold. You could trust gold. He especially liked Krugerrands.

Corazon's minister of treasury pocketed two coins as he counted. Corazon noticed this. Corazon felt good. He was an honest treasurer. A thief would have stolen fifteen coins. There were stories about men who stole nothing, but they were just stories, Corazon knew. The gringos stole also, he knew. But they seemed to have it better organized, so you never saw the coins disappear while they explained they were really trying to help you.

"For you," said Corazon, "we will execute a rapist right before your eyes with my great powers."

"We wait anxiously," said Dr. Jameson. "Being somewhat of an expert on the subject of voodoo, although not of course such an authority as your excellency, we have never heard of a 'protector spirit' such as the one in your box." Dr. Jameson smiled.

"The white man's powers are one thing, the black's and brown's are another. That is why you no understand. I do not understand this atomic bomb of yours and you do not understand my protector spirit," said Corazon, who had coined the phrase when the Russians had been there earlier that morning for their demonstration.

"Bring on the vicious rapist that he may taste the vengeance of his community. Yes?"

Dr. Jameson's delegation eased the minicameras and microinstruments out of their pockets. Sometimes, with an unsophisticated device in its early stages, its very design might divulge its secrets.

Generalissimo Corazon kept the machine under a blue velvet drape at his left beside the gilded Presidential throne chair, which was set on a small platform.

The vicious rapist turned out to be a middle-aged black woman with a red bandana and an orange dress.

"Excuse me," announced Corazon. "We did the rapist this morning. That one is guilty of arch treason and plotting to blow up Ciudad Natividado and other horrible things."

The woman spat.

"Sir," whispered an aide into Jameson's ear. "That's the madam of the whorehouse. She's a second cousin to the Generalissimo. Why would he be killing her on that obviously trumped-up charge?"

Corazon watched the gringo aide whisper in the gringo ear and he had a question of his own. Criminals were one thing. But a second cousin who also had some control with spirits and who sent some of her brothel profits to El Presidente was another.

"Why we kill Juanita?" asked Corazon.

"She was making magic against you," said the new minister of justice.

"What kind?"

"Mountain magic. Saying you are a dead man."

"A lie," said Corazon.

"Yes. Most yes," said the minister. "You are all-powerful. Yes."

Corazon squinted at Juanita. She knew her women and she knew her men. She knew her magic. Was this some strange game? Did she say it at all? Should he ask her? Wouldn't she lie?

Corazon thought deeply about these things and finally he summoned her to him. Two soldiers held her wrists at the end of chains. They followed her.

Corazon leaned forward and whispered into his second cousin's ear.

"Say, Juanita, what is this they tell me about you, that you make the magic against me, heh?"

One of the Britons just behind Dr. Jameson eased a dial in his pocket and turned his left shoulder toward Corazon and the woman. Everything being whispered would be picked up by the miniature directional mike

59

built into the small shoulder pad on the left side of his jacket. Even if Corazon did not give Britain the secret of the machine, M.I.5 could break the secret, and that would at least come in handy to show the Generalissimo the power of Great Britain. Something along the lines of "We have ears everywhere."

Juanita whispered something back. And Corazon asked again why she had made magic against him.

And Juanita whispered something else in her cousin's ear.

Generalissimo Sacristo Corazon bolted upright. Instead of the languid snakelike motions of a serpent ready to strike, Corazon himself jumped.

He grabbed the velvet cover from the black box and threw it in the face of his new minister of justice. He spat on the marble floor. He spat on the box. He spat into his cousin Juanita's face.

"Whore," he called her. "I make you into nothing."

"No matter," said the woman. "Nothing, it matters. Nothing. Nothing."

Corazon, not so wild as to forget his greatest enemies were always his closest allies, turned the phony dials he had mounted on the machine. Secret British cameras and other instrumentation among the Jameson party went into action.

"I give you last chance. Last chance. Whose magic is strongest?"

"Not yours. Never yours."

"Goodbye," said Corazon. "And now look at whose magic is strongest."

For a moment Corazon worried. The last time he had used the machine, it had taken too long to thaw the Umibian ambassador. He pressed the control button. The little gasoline engine whirred away, activating the cathode tube by providing electricity. The cathode rays interacted with what the natives called mung and the power was built up. It was released with a crack and a green glow, and the brightly colored orange dress sighed and collapsed over a dark puddle that had been the madam of the finest brothel in Baqia.

"Impressive," said Dr. Jameson. "We would like to join with you, Britain and Baqia, sister islands in a joint defense."

"Liar," boomed Corazon. "Liar, liar, liar. She was a liar. Liar."

"Quite, your excellency, but as to the matter at hand . . ." began Dr. Jameson.

"The matter is a liar died a liar's death, yes?"

"Yes, of course," said Dr. Jameson. He bowed. The British agents bowed and they left the palace. But they did not return immediately to their hotel rooms. They picked up a bit of South African tail, so to speak, and quite neatly they lured the African agents, posing as businessmen, into a side road, where the good old boys from Eton dispensed with the former colonial Afrikaaners.

Not much to make ado about, Dr. Jameson realized. You allowed the car to follow one of your cars, which led their car into where your chaps waited, and when they slowed to surround your stalled car, some very effective chaps from your show put on a rather neat display of Walther P-38 bullets into their foreheads. Jameson and his men had done it scores of times before, not only to enemy agents but to those of friendly countries—Americans, Israelis, French, Canadians. It didn't matter. The only immorality in spying was being caught.

"Good show," Dr. Jameson told his men.

A South African, dying from a grazing miss that had taken off his left ear, raised a hand for mercy.

He held onto the steering wheel of one of the ambushed cars as if it were life itself.

"So sorry, old boy," said Dr. Jameson. "Cartwright, would you please?"

"'Course," said a bony-faced man. He was a bit sorry he had missed the first time. He put the fellow away with a .38 slug into the right eyeball, which popped like a grape pierced by a javelin. The head went back across the front seat as though yanked by snap pulleys.

It was neat, but then Dr. Jameson had put this unit together in a neat and proper manner. A simple ambush was not about to put anyone out of sorts.

They had worked at their craft with British pluck and a reasonableness so absent from that island's politics or journalism, and so had become that very rare thing: competent. Cartwright turned off the South African's motor.

"What say we do our readouts on the instruments here?" said Dr. Jameson. "The delays from using laboratories back home are really not worth it. Who wants to wait a month to find out that some chambermaid who handled something had tuberculosis or something, what?"

These questions were not really questions. That so-casual air Dr. Jameson had learned to affect encouraged success rather than heroism, and asking a question instead of giving an order kept the whole thing in proportion. No one on his M.I.5 team was about to say no or maybe to any of Dr. Jameson's questions.

The first readout was from the directional listening device.

"Be nice to find out what the brown-berry bugger got so frothed about, what?" said Dr. Jameson.

Corazon spoke in Spanish to his cousin and she in island Spanish to him. It was not the finest Castilian and had overlays of Indian words.

Corazon surprisingly had given his cousin a chance to live. All she had to do was to acknowledge that his power was the greatest on the island. And even more surprisingly, she refused to do this on the grounds that she and Corazon were dead anyhow and why bother. Dr. Jameson shook his head. He couldn't quite believe what the translator had just told him.

One of his crew, the expert on local culture, pointed out that the people of Baqia were quite fatalistic, especially the holy people connected with the island's voodoo religion.

"Give me a literal on that," said Dr. Jameson. He filled a small pipe with a stiff Dunhill mixture. The aide rewound the small tape recorder attached to the directional mike. He talked in English, translating the island Spanish.

"Juanita says 'You dead and to die. Your force weak. You little boy. *Mimado*.' That means spoiled brat. 'You trumpet big things. But you no big thing. You steal president's chair. When big thing and you come together, you lose.' Corazon says, 'Don't say that.' And she says, 'Real power on this island be with the force in the mountain. With the religion of our people. With the voodoo. With the undead. The holy man up there, he be one big power. He gonna be king. And now another big power come and he going make the holy man in the mountains king. And you going to lose.' Something like that. Not clear. And Corazon says, 'You got one more chance,' and she

63

says, 'You got no chance at all,' and then, of course, he does in the poor old thing."

"Wonder," said Dr. Jameson, "who is this man in the hills? And what is this other man, this other force that's going to make the man in the hills king? And why didn't she tell him what he wanted to hear?"

"I think it would be like denying her religion," said the aide.

"Seems strange," said Dr. Jameson. "Dying probably denies her religion, too. She should have just told the mad bugger anything he wanted to be told."

"Not their culture, sir. This is voodoo. This is spirits. A smaller spirit acknowledges a greater spirit and the worst thing that can happen is that a smaller spirit does not acknowledge its relative weakness. That apparently is what Corazon has done. He's failed to acknowledge the supremacy of this holy man in the mountains. His cousin refused to commit the same thing."

"Seems strange," said Jameson. "I'd rather be an apostate than a puddle."

"Would you?" said the aide. "Would we? Why do we risk our lives in this work rather than tend shop or something in Surrey, sir? Why is running over to the enemy and getting rewarded handsomely something that just isn't done?"

"Well, ummm," said Dr. Jameson. "Just not done."

"Precisely. It's our taboo, sir. And denying their voodoo is theirs. So there it is."

"You culture people are bonkers. You make the most absurd thing sound logical," said Dr. Jameson.

"One person's heroism is another person's insanity," said the aide. "It all depends on the culture."

Dr. Jameson waved the man to silence. Legends bothered him. They confused things. Instrumentation, on the other hand, was the great solver of life's puzzles.

Corazon had showed them the machine and, with the miniaturized instruments hidden on their bodies, they had recorded its power and its sounds and its waves.

The conclusion of the experts—"just rough, of course, sir"—was that at the point of impact, a rearranging signal was sent to the cells in the human body. In other words, the cells rearranged themselves.

"In other words?" said Dr. Jameson. "I haven't followed a bloody word."

"The machine sends out a signal that triggers matter to alter itself. Organic matter. Living matter."

"Good. Then if we have the signal we can make the bloody machine ourselves."

"Not quite, sir. The types of rays and waves in the world are infinite. The triggering device in Corazon's machine is probably some substance we know nothing about."

"Then how did that savage in medals figure it out?"

"He probably just lucked into it," said one of the scientific members of the team. "Just a guess, until we get lab reports, but I think the machine works off the human nervous system. That poor woman's dress was cotton. That was organic material. But it was unaffected."

"I felt a bit woozy, sir," offered the youngest member of Jameson's team. "When the machine went on, I felt woozy."

"Anyone else?" asked Dr. Jameson.

They had felt tingles. Only one man had felt nothing, and that was Dr. Jameson himself.

"You had a spot of brandy before our meeting, sir," offered an aide.

"Yes. True," said Jameson.

"And there was that Umibian. We heard that Corazon had to hit him twice with the rays before he went. He was drunk as a lord, sir."

"Nervous system. Alcohol. Perhaps," said Dr. Jameson. "Perhaps we could assault the presidential palace roaring drunk, eh? And then we'd be immune to the machine."

The men chuckled. Unfortunately things were not that simple. The whole island, especially the capital of Ciudad Natividado, was seething with foreign operations. One might successfully get his hands on the machine, losing quite a few men in the process, but then be too weak to get it out of the country. Because all the other agents seeing one with the prize would join together to thwart the winner. Whoever got the machine first would have to fight a mini world war. Alone.

Dr. Jameson had grown to love this keen working group of effective killers. They could get on with the dirty work and leave it behind. He would match his stout band against anyone else. But not against everyone else. The odds were just too great.

It was a weird island, this. And a weirder situation. The key to a situation with so many weird variables was to stay orderly and not try to match weird with weird, witch doctor with witch doctor, but just stay with what you knew. Keep the British square, so to speak. Let the others make the mistakes. Yes. Dr. Jameson sucked on his pipe and watched the scrub and palm whiz by his window on the dirt road.

Had Corazon stumbled onto some sort of magic? The dials on the machine were not all functioning. Unless, of course, the most destructive machine ever invented used parts from a Waring blender and a spring-motor from an Erector set.

In Ciudad Natividado, the British point man reported that their room in the hotel had been occupied by an aged Oriental and a skinny white man who, when confronted with the working end of a Walther P-38, replied that he wasn't that happy with the island, his own government, any other government, the day, the hotel, the man pointing the gun, or the taped soap opera blaring out of a television set that had been brought to play the tape, which he had seen twenty-two times and didn't like the first time, either. However, if the British agent wanted to do himself a favor, he would not interrupt the show. Especially since in this heat, he would also be doing the white man a favor because the white man didn't feel like disposing of bodies, but in this heat you couldn't just let them lie around.

Yes, the white man had responded further, he was aware it was a pistol being pointed at his face and, no, he did not know it was a Walther whatchamacallit and it made no difference whether the man intended to shoot or not.

"Say anything else?" Dr. Jameson asked.

"Yes, sir. He didn't like those drums beating all the time either."

"Sounds like a nit," said Dr. Jameson over the radio.

"Yes, sir."

"Well, remove them from the room, if you would."

"By force?"

"Why not?"

"Yes, sir. Kill?"

"If you have to," radioed Jameson.

"It is for a room, sir. Only a room."

"On Baqia, that is enough."

"They look so defenseless, sir. Not a weapon on them. And the white man *is* an American, sir."

"It's been a hard day," said Dr. Jameson. "Please." And he waited in his car, with the rest of his team in their cars, for the word that the room had been cleared out. When twenty minutes had passed, Dr. Jameson sent another man with a radio transmitter that worked and told him to report back that indeed the room had been cleared out, and if the first agent's radio had failed to work properly there would be what-ho in the supply room back in London.

The second agent did not return, either.

CHAPTER FOUR

Remo looked at the pistol. There was a way a man cradled a pistol butt that was a fairly certain indication of when the trigger would be pulled.

Most people tended not to notice these things, because when you are looking at someone you think is about to kill you, the perceptions of trigger fingers and how the ridges of the skin rest on the gunmetal trigger just aren't there. Unless they were trained to be there. It was like hitting a baseball with a bat. It would be an impossible thing for someone who had never seen a baseball come at him before, but it was just a regular occurrence for a major leaguer who had hit baseball after baseball.

So Remo knew the man wasn't about to pull the trigger because he just wasn't ready for it. The pressure of the finger ridges wasn't there.

"Yeah, okay, thank you for the threat and come back when you're ready to kill," Remo said.

Remo shut the door.

Chiun sat lotus-position before the television set. Old actors were young again on this television screen, brought down to Baqia from the States in the luggage along with the tapes. Chiun did not like the modern soap operas. When sex and violence began to appear, he called it blasphemy and refused to watch the new shows. So he had taken to rewatching what he called "the only redeeming thing in your culture, your one great art form."

For a time, Chiun had tried to write his own soap opera, but he had spent so much time working on the title, the dedication, and the speech he would make when he received an Emmy that he never quite got around to writing the script. It was one of the things that Remo never mentioned to him.

"What is wrong with love and concern and marriage?" Chiun asked.

He answered himself. "Nothing," he said.

Now he mouthed the words of Dr. Channing Murdoch Callaher telling Rebecca Wentworth her mother was dying of a rare disease and that he felt he couldn't operate on the mother because he knew who Rebecca's real father was.

The organ music heightened the drama. Chiun's lips ceased to move as a commercial for a soap powder came on. It advertised that it had more zyclomite than any other cleaner. Remo knew the commercial was old, because modern commercials advertised that cleansers were zyclomite free.

"Who was at the door?" asked Chiun during the commercial.

"Nobody," said Remo. "Some British guy."

"Never speak ill of the British. Henry the Eighth always paid on time and purchased regularly. Good and noble Henry was a blessing to his people and a pride to his race. He showed that no matter how funny a person's eyes were, he could still show that he had a Korean heart."

"You know what you're going to do here?" asked Remo.

"Yes," said Chiun.

"What?"

"See what happens to Rebecca," Chiun said.

"Rebecca?" asked Remo, shocked. "Rebecca lives for seven more years, has fourteen major operations, three abortions, becomes an astronaut, a political investigator, a congressperson, gets a hysterectomy, and then gets raped, shot at, and inherits a department store before her contract with her studio runs out, whereupon she is run over by a faulty truck that was supposed to be recalled to Detroit."

Chiun's eyes moved slowly, as if searching for someone to share his shock at such a dastardly deed as destroying many many hours of what a poor, delicate kind gentle soul took his small pleasures in. There was no one else in the room but an ungrateful pupil.

"Thank you," said Chiun. His voice was laden with hurt.

There was a knock at the door again. The Briton in the blue blazer, light summer slacks, and the dandy Walther P-38 was at the door. This time the finger was closed on the trigger and the butt was set to take the slight kick. He was ready to kill.

"I'm afraid, old boy, you're just going to have to toodleoo off, what?"

"No," said Remo. "We just got here."

"I really don't want to kill you, you know. A bit of a mess."

"Don't worry. You're not going to kill anybody."

"I *am* pointing the gun directly at your head, you know."

"I know," said Remo. He rested one hand against the doorjamb.

Chiun glanced over at the intruder at the door. Not only was his joy with the show spoiled by the revelation of the next six-hundred episodes, of which four-hundred were absolutely the best, but now Remo was going to put a body in the room while the main show was going on. He wasn't going to wait until the next commercial, Chiun knew. And why? Why would Remo kill that man at the door during the show, instead of waiting until a commercial?

Chiun knew the answer.

"Hater of beauty," he snapped at Remo.

The British agent took a tentative step back. "I don't think you realize with whom you're dealing," he said.

"That's your problem, not ours," Remo said.

"You're a dead man, you know," said the agent. He had the forehead of this casual American directly in line with his gunsights. He would blast out the frontal lobe with such force there probably would be a king-sized hole in the back of the head, also.

"He's gonna shoot, Little Father. You hear him? He's gonna shoot now. It's not my fault."

"Beauty hater," said Chiun viciously.

"If you'll bother to look, you'll see his hand is gonna move that gun. Any moment now, he's gonna squeeze that trigger."

"Any moment now," said Chiun in a whiny, imitative voice, "he's going to squeeze the trigger. He's going to squeeze the trigger. So let's all interrupt anything that's going on because he's going to squeeze the trigger."

The agent had waited long enough. He did not understand why these two so casually faced death. Nor was he all that concerned. He had killed many men before and sometimes there was a dumb disbelief on the part of the victim. At other times fear. But never casual cattiness like between these two. Still there was a first time for anything.

He squeezed the trigger. The Walther P-38 jumped in his hand. But he did not feel the kick. And the white man's forehead was still there. All of it. Unpunctured. What wasn't there was the Walther P-38 or his hand. At his wrist, there was the incredible wrenching like a giant tooth being taken out of his arm. He had felt force but no pain.

And he hadn't seen the man's hands move. He did catch a glimpse of a finger moving between his two eyes and he could have sworn he had seen it go in up to the fist knuckle of that hand and it was like a very big door had slammed on his head. He could have sworn that. But he wasn't swearing anymore. His last thought was a memory and by the time his body hit the floor he was not feeling anything.

His nerve endings were sending messages, but that part of the brain that was to receive them had been traumatized into a loose bloody pudding.

Remo wiped his finger off on the man's shirt and stacked him neatly in front of the room with the Bulgarians in it. A Kalishnikov assault rifle poked its way out of the door.

Someone asked a question in Russian, then French, and finally English.

"Who you?"

73

"Me me," answered Remo, covering the forehead mess of the British agent with the straw skimmer.

"Who me?" came the voice from behind the partially opened door.

"You you," said Remo.

"No, you," said the voice.

"Me?" asked Remo.

"Yes. Why you?"

"Me me. You you," said Remo.

"What you do out there?"

"I'm putting a body away because the air conditioning doesn't work and they tend to stink after a while.

"Why at our door?"

"Why not at your door?"

Remo thought that was a good answer. Obviously whoever was behind the door did not because he fired off a burst from the Kalishnikov.

Back in the room, Chiun noted gunfire down the hall, which did not help the drama.

"Sorry," said Remo.

Chiun gave a nod, but not one that accepted Remo's excuse. It was a nod that acknowledged that Remo, one way or another, had found and always would find a way to trifle with an old man's pleasure. And sure enough, Remo did again with another Englishman and, this time, two shots into the room and a hand grenade down the hall.

This disturbance not entirely ruining Chiun's afternoon, Remo then announced that he saw a whole team coming around the building. They all wore blazers and straw skimmers. Their leader was a man with a pipe.

"Isn't it interesting that we are attacked always

74

while Rebecca is making her most beautiful speeches?" Chiun said.

"They attack when they attack, Little Father," Remo said.

"No doubt," said Chiun.

"They really are," said Remo.

The groups had come in what was known as a reserve triangle. Up the front of the street, up an alley on the side, and with two triangle tops, which was two men on each side, two men frontal and two behind them.

It was a really good team, Remo estimated. They moved together. They obviously had worked together before. You could tell that by the coordination without many commands. New people were always shouting or signaling to each other or running off in different directions. Remo took a position on the roof so he could see how each group came on. A dark man wielding two heavy .44s stared nervously around. He didn't know who to defend against first. He cursed in Russian and backed off into a corner.

Remo saw two skimmered heads go into the front of the building while another pair threw a grappling ladder to the window sill of Chiun's room and two in the alley started up a fire escape.

"Just working," Remo said to the man with the two .44s. "You stay there."

Chiun had taught him that when working multiples it was always best to concentrate on something that had no direct relationship to the action of the multiples. Like breathing. Remo concentrated on the breathing and let his body take care of the other work. He was out over the ledge of the building and down along the side, slapping at each sill and keeping the rhythm of his inner lungs aligned with the breath itself, when he met the two coming up the grappling hook line to Chiun's window.

"Oh," said one, going back down to the dusty alley alongside the hotel. The other's Walther was rendered useless by going buttfirst through his own sternum, creating great problems for the heart, which found gun handles even more hazardous than cholesterol.

Across the street, peering out a slight crack in the Venetian blinds in one of the upper rooms, Generalissimo Sacristo Corazon saw the thin white man come down off the roof and knew, without anyone telling him, that his cousin Juanita had been telling the truth about a stronger power than his.

He had never seen a man drop like that. He had seen bodies fall from buildings. He had even seen divers jump off cliffs in Mexico. And once he had seen a plane blow up in the air.

But this white man. He dropped faster than someone falling. He dropped faster than someone in a dive. It looked as if he had harnessed gravity to enable himself to go down a wall faster than was normal.

The white man's body cleaned the rope of the two men like two exposed peas being flicked from an open pod.

"Who? Who that man?" demanded Corazon, pointing through the Venetian blind toward Remo.

"A white man," offered a major. He had a .44-caliber pistol in his holster, identical to Corazon's. His father had been in the hills with Corazon's father. When the senior Corazon had become President, the major's father had refused to be promoted to general. He died an old man. The lesson was not lost on his son, whose name was Manuel Estrada. When the young Corazon became El Presidente for life, Manuel

Estrada also refused to be promoted to general. He also hoped to have a long life. But unlike his father, he planned one day to have everything.

The senior Estrada had had a family motto. It was "Nobody ever got shot for being a little thief." Manuel Estrada had a motto, too. It was "Wait your turn."

Major Estrada was just about the only man in the entourage whose hands did not sweat when Corazon was near. He had high cheekbones that showed his Indian blood and wine dark skin that showed his African. His nose was proud, a reminder of the night a Castilian bedded a slave brought to work the sugar.

He heard Corazon scream at him that anyone could see it was a white man, but from what country was this white man?

"A white country," said Estrada.

"What white country? Find out. Find out now, Estrada, now."

Corazon watched Remo move along the front of the Astarse Hotel. His movements looked like a shuffle and appeared slow, until you realized the movement of the limbs might be slow but not of the body itself. It was moving almost in a blur. It went into the two Britishers like water through a ball of sand.

Remo's feet raised no dust. Corazon muttered. It was the strange power Juanita spoke of.

He uttered some prayers. "Lord, remove this evil thing from our blessed island. In your son's name, we humbly pray, so you do this little thing for us."

These words did the chief of state utter, looking down at Remo. He was still there. Well, if prayers to the Lord didn't work, a good holy man had other tricks.

"Power of darkness and stench of the devil, bring-

77

ing down on men a curse eternal, land on that one there."

Corazon saw the white man take on two more Britishers. Looked like he could dodge bullets, too.

Corazon spat on the palace floor. "To hell with both of you," he said. It was like dealing with superpowers who were intent on ignoring him. What good were gods anyway if they didn't listen to you?

Suddenly the man stumbled. "Thank you, Beelzebub," said Corazon, but it wasn't a stumble. Remo had slid sideways to move off into the back of the alley. Corazon cursed his gods again.

That was the problem with too many people today, he thought. They were afraid to punish their gods. But he kept reminding them that if they messed around with Sacristo Corazon he wasn't going to fall down on his knees, saying, "I love you, anyhow." What was he supposed to be, some kind of Irishman? You messed with Corazon, god, forget it. You don't get so much as a candle.

But that was with Western gods. There was one god that Corazon did not call on. It was the god of the wind and the night and the cold and it lived in the hills and in its honor those voodoo drums beat twenty-four hours a day, and Corazon did not call on that god because he was afraid of it. Even more than he was afraid of this force . . . this white man across the street.

He had his own force. He had the machine. Like any commander, he knew his limits. Even with a great weapon. After a battle, everyone says you won because you had the great weapon. But before the battle, you must consider what happens if you use your great weapon and it does not work.

Nothing was worse than pointing a gun at someone's head and hearing a click because the chamber was empty.

What if his machine did not work against the new force?

Juanita had said the new force would triumph and bring kinghood to the holy man of the mountains.

And just that very day, the Umibian delegate had gotten two full doses from Corazon's machine before he had collapsed.

The machine was losing power, he had thought. But Juanita had gone quickly. Did the machine still work the way it should or not? Corazon had to think carefully before he used it. He could not afford to aim, fire, and leave someone standing. Then, even if he did live, which was doubtful, all the money would go. The embassies would return to lazy one-man operations. The ships would leave the harbor and Baqia would be almost as bad as before the Spanish came.

One did not use one's major weapon lightly. But how to use it? When Corazon was thinking, he liked to have a woman. When he was thinking deeply, he liked to have two women. Very deeply, three. And so on.

When the fifth woman had left his private rooms, which were a minifortress within the fortresslike presidential palace compound, Corazon knew what he would do.

Major Estrada had the Britisher, Dr. Jameson, in tow. Dr. Jameson was still in a state of shock.

"I don't believe it. I don't believe it," he gasped.

"Who was that man who did those awful things to your people?"

"I don't believe it," Jameson gasped. He sucked on the pipestem, which was now minus a bowl. He had lost his entire crew. It was impossible. No one man

79

could do that. And besides, what would M.I.5 say about the lost instrumentation? This was hardly a neat operation.

"Who was that man?"

"American."

Corazon thought about this. With any other country that had a force like that, you would give respect. But Americans, he had learned, could be made ashamed of their force. They could be made helpless. Americans like to be abused. Quadruple the price of a raw material and they would hold conferences at their own expense to explain to the world that you had a God-given right to that raw material and so could set any price you wanted. They had forgotten what everyone else knew. Force gained you respect. America was insane.

If it had been the Russians who had that force with them, Corazon would have gone directly to the Russians, run the hammer and sickle up the Baqian flagpoles, and declared his everlasting friendship.

But you didn't do that with Americans. When America or any of its allies used force, it became the focus of ill will at the United Nations. People from all over condemned the U.S. warmongers. As the Russian had reminded Corazon today:

"Be a full-fledged member of the Third World, supporting us in everything, and you can't commit a crime. Only America and friends of America can commit crimes. And we can give you two hundred American professors swearing you are being picked on unfairly if you should ever have to start a real bloodbath. And we're the only ones still making gas ovens for human disposal. And no one says a word."

The Russian pointed out that good, safe governments had to kill all the time. It was the only sure way of getting respect. With communism, one could do it free of criticism. And never have to hold an election.

Now Corazon did not like Russians as people, but as a leader one had to make sacrifices.

"Break the relations with America," said Corazon.

"What?" asked Major Estrada.

"Break the relations with America and bring me the Russian ambassador."

"I don't know how to break the relations with a country."

"Do I have to do everything?"

"All right. When?" asked Corazon.

"Now," said Corazon.

"Anything else?"

Corazon shook his head. "It is big thing, breaking the relations with a country. People read this to me all the time."

"Who reads?" asked Estrada.

"The minister of education. He reads."

"He's a good reader," admitted Estrada. He had seen him read for an audience once. The minister of education had gotten through a big fat book with no pictures in one short afternoon. Once, Estrada had asked a so-called smart American how fast he had read that book and the so-called smart American said it had taken him a week. Baqia had a good minister of education.

"Another thing," said Corazon. "Take care of this man here." He nodded to the dazed Dr. Jameson.

"Bring him to the British consul?" asked Estrada.

"No," said Corazon.

"Oh," said Estrada, and with his .44 put two thumping slugs into the blue blazer. One of the slugs blew the breast patch off the jacket.

81

"Not here, *stupido*," yelled Corazon. "I want him shoot here, I shoot him here myself."

"You say take care of him. You say break the relations with America. You say get Russian ambassador and get him here. Hey, what's all this, eh? I got one afternoon."

"Anybody else as stupid as you, Estrada, I shoot."

"You can't shoot me," said Estrada, putting his smoking pistol back in the holster.

"Why not?" demanded Corazon. He didn't like hearing a thing like that.

"Because I the only one you know who won't shoot you if I get a chance."

The Russian ambassador perspired profusely. He rubbed his hands. He wore a very floppy suit. He was a middle-aged man and had served as a consul in Chile, Ecuador, Peru, and now here in Baqia. He had his own ratings for countries, on a scale of one to ten. Ten being the most likely to get killed in. He didn't mind living for socialism but he certainly didn't want to die for it. He rated Baqia at twelve.

He had three children and a wife at home in Sverdlovsk. He had a sixteen-year-old dark-eyed island beauty here in Baqia. He didn't want to go home.

When he heard the Generalissimo wanted to see him, he didn't know if it was for his own execution, someone else's execution, or just a request to give more help to another Third World country aspiring to break the chains of colonialism, which was just another word for a shakedown. The Russian ambassador was Anastas Bogrebyan. He was of Armenian descent. He had one purpose on this island and that was to oversee all operations aimed at getting the device that disintegrated people, and failing that to make sure no one else got it. On important scientific matters that had to be done right, the Russians now sent Armenians. It used to be Jews, but too many kept right on going once outside Russia.

"I love Russia and communism and socialism and all that stuff," Corazon told the ambassador. "And I am thinking what can I do for my Russian friends, I am thinking?"

Corazon tapped the blue velvet drape over the special machine. Bogrebyan had dealt with natives before. He knew he wasn't going to get this machine right away. Not without bargaining.

"What is the very best thing I can give my friends, the Russians?"

Bogrebyan shrugged. Was it really possible he was going to give the machine itself to Russia? No, it was impossible. Even though he was hearing what he was hearing, Bogrebyan did not think Corazon was the kind of man to surrender so easily what he knew was the only thing that was pumping money into his country. Moreover, this man who had lived all his life by stealth and death was not about to panic into giving something away when he could put on the squeeze. And then Bogrebyan saw the squeeze.

Corazon announced he was breaking diplomatic relations with America, but he was afraid.

"Afraid of what?" asked Bogrebyan.

"What America will do to me. Will you protect me?"

"Of course. We love you," said Bogrebyan, knowing there was more to come.

"There are American CIA killer agent spies here, on my sacred soil of Baqia."

"There is no place of value that does not have spies from everywhere, comrade," said Bogrebyan shrewdly. He had a honker of a nose with a few small hairs on the end of it. Perspiration collected on the hairs. But Bogrebyan's soul was cool.

Corazon grinned. He had a round face like a big dark melon.

"You protect us?" he said.

"What do you want?"

"I want Americans dead. Over there. In the Astarse. Americans, yes?"

"Perhaps," said Bogrebyan. "But we want something in return. We want to help you use your new device for the good of all mankind. For peaceful purposes. For us."

Corazon knew he had been outmaneuvered, but he was not about to give up.

"Or I might join those killers over there. In the Astarse. Throw myself at their mercy. It can happen."

Now Bogrebyan wondered why Corazon himself could not take care of the Americans. Cautiously he said, "We'll see. There are many, many spies here now. We are not quite sure, comrade, why you fear these two."

"Comrade," said Corazon, embracing the Russian. "Get them, you get my magic." But in his heart the great fear was growing. It was possible the Russians would fail. "Do not fail," Corazon blurted. "Use enough men and do not fail."

In the evening he went to his window overlooking the Astarse. He waited for the Russians. They would be coming soon. Bogrebyan was not a stupid man. The sun set red down Baqian Route 1. He saw the Russians then, down the road, strolling quite casually. Twenty-five men with guns and ropes and light mortars. All pretenses were gone. It was going to be a war.

Corazon's heart beat with a dash of joy now. It might work. It might very well work, he thought.

He had heard among other things that morning that one of the lower officers who worked at the airport said there was an old Oriental one should be afraid of who was part of the American team. Old men died quicker when helped to their deaths. And then to his further joy Corazon, peering from the palace window, saw that another equally strong group of Russians were coming from the other direction on Route 1.

The Russians were pulling out all the stops. The melon face had a big white-toothed wedge of a smile from ear to ear. Corazon would have sung the Russian national anthem if he had known it.

He saw heads peer out windows in the Astarse. He saw the same heads disappear. He saw men jump out windows. Run out through the alley limping. The Astarse was clearing like a sink of roaches when the light was suddenly turned on. Some men left their weapons.

The Russians began to chant, smelling their triumph. A bold move. A strong move. Corazon knew that when you dealt with Russians, you dealt with action. But nothing like this had he expected.

One little old man in a gown stood at a window in the Astarse. He was in the second floor. He had wisps of white hair, Corazon noticed, as he looked more closely. His arms were folded over themselves. And Corazon saw it was not a robe he wore but a light blue garment from the Orient. He had seen them before.

Corazon made out the features in the fast-failing light. The old man was an Oriental. He looked up the street and smiled, and then down the street and smiled.

He was smiling at the Russians. And it was the smile of a man who had just been offered an interesting dessert.

And then with horror Corazon realized the full meaning of that smile. The Oriental thought of Russia's major attacking forces as mere amusement. The calm look was not the ignorance of an old man but contentment, the confidence of a melon chopper who had chopped melon all day and was not about to be excited by a few more.

The Oriental looked up, across the street into the presidential palace, and caught Corazon's eyes. And very quietly, he smiled again.

Corazon ducked behind the Venetian blinds. In his own palace, in his own country, he was afraid to look out of his own window. He knew what would happen.

"Juanita," he muttered to the soul of the dead. "If you are around, I acknowledge your rightness."

CHAPTER FIVE

Major Manuel Estrada broke relations with America
as well as he could. But first he had to get rid of the
Englishman's body, then get one of the cleaning
people to clean up the blood in the Generalissimo's
receiving room, then find some people to bury the
body, and, of course, to share the knowledge of these
heavy burdens with his friends at the cantina.

Somehow the cantina got into the work mix before
some of the other duties, and when he left the cantina, it was dark and someone was lying drunk in the
middle of Route 1. Estrada kicked the man.

"Get up, drunken man," said Estrada. "You foolish
drunken thing. Do you not have things to do? Foolish
drunken man."

Estrada tripped over him from a standing position.
Then he felt the man's face. It was cold. The man of
course was dead. Estrada apologized to the man for
calling him a drunkard. Then Estrada noticed the

blue blazer and the head wound. It was Dr. Jameson, the Englishman.

Estrada pushed his hands at air. While others might not understand what this meant, Estrada did. He was abandoning this job for now. He had more important things to do.

Let the dead bury the dead, someone had once said. He knew that man who said that was a pretty smart man. It was Jesus in the Bible. And Jesus was God. Therefore, it would be a sin for Major Manuel Estrada, the living, to bury the dead. It would be a sin against Jesus. And it was not good to be a sinful man.

So let Dr. Jameson lie.

The American Embassy was a modern sprawling aluminum and concrete structure that someone once told Major Estrada represented an Indian prayer in tangible form. It was to show America's and Baqia's common Indian heritage. Two peoples, one future.

Now Manuel Estrada might not be the smartest man on the island. But he knew that when someone told you that you and he had something in common, he wanted something.

Estrada was always waiting for the Americans to ask for something. He did not trust their generosity. Never had. They never asked for anything, so he resented them. That resentment was going to make the evening's job easier.

He careened to the front door of the embassy and banged on it. A well-dressed American marine in formal blue pants and khaki shirt festooned with medals opened the door.

Estrada demanded to see the ambassador. He had a message from El Presidente, Generalissimo Sacristo

Corazon himself, for the ambassador himself. The ambassador rushed to the door.

The ambassador, no slouch at island politics, had monitored the Russian buildup. He knew they had made some sort of deal with Corazon.

"You," said Estrada.

"Yes?" said the ambassador. He was in his bathrobe and slippers.

"Get out this country now. Get out here. Go. We no like you. This breaks the sex."

"What?" asked the ambassador. "Oh, you mean break relations."

"Yeah. That's the thing. Do it and go. Now. Good. Thank you. Very much thank you," said Estrada. "That's the word. Break relations. Broken. Broke. Done. Forever. We don't want see you round here forever. But don't worry, American. These things never last. *Hasta luego.* Let us drink to our separation. You leave the embassy liquor. We watch it for you."

In America, the news was received solemnly. There could be little doubt any longer that the Russians had gotten hold of the secret machine that could make a major war an easy victory.

The national commentator who had earlier seen Baqia's wavering as a sign of an absence of moral leadership by America now said this was further evidence "that if we're going to rely on ships and guns we're not going to make it."

The commentator appeared on national television several nights a week and did not know what an army was, did not know how things got done, and still believed America had kept a foreign country out of a war by slipping one of the leaders a million dollars.

Which was like stopping a Mafia hit by offering the button man a gift of milk and cookies. In any other country at any other time, the commentator would have been politely humored. In America he was heard by multimillions.

The President listened to him. He did not, like anyone else who knew what was going on in the world, respect the man. But he did know that the commentator, while never being a good newsman, was an excellent propagandist.

Something had gone wrong in Baqia. The President waited for the proper time and was at his room with the special red telephone to CURE.

"What is going on in Baqia?" the President asked.

"I don't know, sir," came back the acid voice of Dr. Harold W. Smith.

"We're getting our heads handed to us. Those boys are supposed to be good. And they haven't done anything. Call 'em off."

"You assigned them, sir," Smith reminded him.

"I don't need an I-told-you-so at this point."

"I was not being sarcastic, sir. You have made an arrangement with Sinanju, sir. They are not like civil servants. Before Rome existed as a city, sir, Sinanju already had an elaborate procedure for ending service to an emperor."

"What is it?"

"I am not exactly sure," said Smith.

"You mean you took it upon yourself to hire a killer and can't get rid of? Because you don't know the correct procedure?"

"No, sir, we did not. Emphatically we did not. Sinanju was entered into contract to train one of our men. We never agreed to unleash the Master of

90

Sinanju. We have never done it. *You* did it. For the first time."

"Well, what happens now?"

"I would advise you to let that person work out what he is going to work out. Surprisingly, in international politics not much has changed since the Ming dynasty. It may go wrong. But I would bet that it will probably go right down there."

"I don't bet. Give me guarantees."

"There are none," Smith said.

"Thanks for nothing," said the President. He rammed the red telephone into the back of the bureau drawer. He stormed out of the bedroom and down to his business offices in the White House. He wanted the Central Intelligence Agency and wanted them now and he would cut any orders the CIA wanted. He wanted CIA presence in Baqia. Now.

Delicately, the CIA director explained that he had fourteen bound volumes in his office that would prove that the CIA couldn't do what the President wanted. His message, in essence, was "Don't ask." We may not know what's going on in the world and we may embarrass you often and we may rarely succeed in foreign adventures, but baby, back here in Washington where it counts, we know how to play it safe, and nobody messes with us.

The President's response, in essence, was "Do it or I'll have your ass."

"But our image, Mr. President."

"To hell with your image. Protect the country."

"Which one, sir?"

"The one you work for, you idiot. Now do it."

"I'll need it in writing."

Now, since it was a direct order and since the President was going to commit himself in writing, and since the CIA could always explain later to columnists and congressmen that they had not gone into this thing on their own but were pushed, it was somewhat safe to go ahead.

Times like these were dangerous. First, they must not be accused of using illegal force, even though those who were most likely to make the charge were America's enemies. Secondly and probably equally important, the CIA must not be accused of discrimination.

Thus, after careful analysis, it came down to one agent as the only person who could safely protect the CIA in times like these.

"Hey, Ruby. It fo' you. It some Washington fella."

Ruby Jackson Gonzalez looked up from a bill of lading. She had opened this small wig factory in Norfolk, Virginia, because that was where she could buy human hair cheapest. The sailors off the ships brought her duffel bags of it from around the world. The business was thriving.

She also had a very healthy government check each month—$2,283.53—which came to more than $25,000 a year clear for just signing the checks.

At twenty-two, Ruby had enough smarts to know the government didn't pay her all that money for a smile. She had gotten the smarts despite going to New York City public schools.

During Afro-pride classes she smuggled in a McGuffey reader her grandmother had given her and hid it inside the cover of a Malcolm X coloring book given to high school students. She taught herself to write by copying over and over the neatest script she could find. When the school discarded the old mathematics books in favor of new "relevant texts" that concentrated on the complicated concepts of "many" and "not so many," she dug into the big garbage bags and collected a whole set. With those, she taught herself to add, subtract, multiply, and divide and for $5 a week she got some boy from a private school in Riverdale to teach her about equations and logarithms and the calculus.

Thus, at graduation from high school, it was she who was chosen to read each classmate what his or her diploma said.

"Them big words," said one boy. "Ah hope Dartmuff don' speck us to know all them big words."

Ruby had killed a man by the time she was sixteen. In the ghetto there was a horror for young girls that was not spoken of outside. Grown men would sometimes wrestle them into a room for a mass rape. It was called "pulling the train."

Ruby, whose smooth skin looked like light chocolate cream and who had a sharp sudden smile like the opening of a box of candy surprises, could make most men do pleasant double takes. She was attractive and, as her body filled out and she became a woman, she could sense men looking at her in that way. In a different place, it would have been a stroke to one's ego. But in the ghetto of Bedford-Stuyvesant, it could mean finding yourself kidnaped in a room for a day or two and only possibly being able to get out alive.

She carried a small gun. And they got her in school.

She had been so careful, yet it was a girlfriend who tricked her. She was in love with one of the boys, but he fancied Ruby and her lighter skin. So Ruby's friend asked her to come into an empty gym to help her with some work. Ruby moved through the big doors, reinforced to shield the outside from the sound of cheering crowds and grunting players.

A big black hand was over her mouth immediately

and someone was telling her to relax and enjoy it, because if she didn't she'd only hurt herself.

She worked her hand into her panties just before someone ripped them off and had her hand on the little pistol her brother had given her.

She fired once in front and the young man behind her head squeezed harder till she saw blackness and light sparkles. She put the gun right behind her ear and fired. She felt herself fall to the floor. She had been released. She saw a big young man walking, stooped over, holding his right cheek with his hand. Blood flowed down his arm. He was wounded in the cheek. Panicked, he ran into her. And, panicking, Ruby unloaded the gun into his belly. It was small-caliber, but five shots made his intestines into pulp and he died from loss of blood at the hospital. The other boys fled.

Thereafter Ruby Jackson Gonzalez walked the halls as if she went to school in a place where girls were protected.

The boy's death was one of eight shootings that year in the school, down 50 percent from the year before. By this reduction in classroom homicide the principal won a pilot study grant to determine why his school was better able to control crime this year than last. The conclusion of the study group, led by a man who had gotten his Ph.D. in intergroup dynamics, was that the school had better intergroup dynamics that year.

Meanwhile Ruby graduated and when this government job at a phenomenal salary came along she took it. The elaborate CIA cover lasted an hour and a half with her. She knew that the CIA was the only outfit in the country that paid so much for so little, except the Mafia, and she wasn't Italian.

She also had a pretty solid idea of why the CIA would want her. As a woman, a black, and carrying a Spanish surname, she was an entire equal opportunity program for them. She made them look good on the statistics.

It was three wonderful years just collecting checks, but all the while Ruby knew it had to end sometime. There was nothing really free in the world, she knew, and only idiots expected it.

The end came with an afternoon visit by a naval officer familiar enough with her salary scale and employment record to be accepted for what he was, her superior in the organization.

He wanted to talk to her at greater length but they couldn't do it here in her factory on Granby Street in Norfolk, Virginia. Could she come to the naval base that afternoon?

She could, and she didn't return. Like the encounter in the gym back in high school, she had been ambushed. This time by a bureaucracy.

She could, if she wanted, refuse the assignment. No one was forcing her. No one was forcing her, either, to accept those healthy checks each month, the naval officer said. When he explained that the assignment wasn't especially dangerous, something in Ruby told her that her chances were no more than 50-50.

And when he explained that "an American undercover presence must be maintained at a minimal level," she knew it meant that she'd be going in alone. If she got into trouble, don't call them, they'll call you.

That was no matter. She had known all her life that it was her responsibility to protect her own life and that all the help this very good-looking officer promised her wouldn't be worth two spits in a hurricane.

She had never heard of Baqia before. On the plane there, America's intelligence presence at a minimal level asked the passenger in the next seat what Baqia was like.

"It's awful."

The plane landed and Baqia was a madhouse. There was one hotel in the country, called the Astarse. "If you be a spy," said the hotel clerk, "you be right at home here."

And, he said, they had recently had a vacancy because all the occupants in the room had been killed. There were more bodies lying around unburied in this hotel than in a big city morgue.

There was no room service and there was a very big lump in the bed. The lump was a dying man. He spoke Russian.

"How can I use that bed?" demanded Ruby. "There's a man dying in it."

"He be dead," said the clerk. "You wait. We see lot of lung wounds. They always kill. Don't worry you pretty little head."

Ruby went to the window and looked out into the street. Across the dusty road was the presidential palace. In the window directly opposite her was a fat black man looking like an overdressed doorman at a white hotel. He had a lot of medals. He grinned at her and waved.

"Congratulations, sweetheart, chiquita. You now selected as the lover of our sacred leader, Generalissimo Sacristo Corazon, praise his wonderfulness forever. He is the greatest lover of all time."

"He look like a turkey," Ruby said.

"Shut you eyes and pretend you getting a tooth drilled down below. He be over very fast, you don' even know how fast. Then you come back to me for some real loving."

Ruby sensed her survival depended on submitting. She could endure any man, provided it was just one man. And maybe she would luck out, steal Corazon's machine, and be on the next plane home before he knew it was missing.

There was no formal greeting from El Presidente when Ruby entered his sleeping rooms. Corazon was nude except for his pistol belt. He kept a velvet-covered box near the side of his bed.

He acknowledged that he might not be up to par. He had grievous problems. He might have backed the wrong side in an international matter.

Would the beautiful lady, he asked, possibly accept only the second greatest lover in the world, which he was when he was not the greatest, that being when he was not worried about international politics.

"Sure. Go ahead. Get it over with," Ruby said.

"He is over with," said Corazon. He was putting on his riding boots.

"Oh, wonderful," said Ruby. "You're the greatest. My main man. Wowee. That is doing the do. Wow. Some lover."

"You really think so?" asked Corazon.

"Sure," said Ruby. One thing you had to say for the man. He was neat. He didn't even leave moisture.

"You like the Astarse Hotel?" asked Corazon.

"No," said Ruby. "But it will do."

"You meet anybody there? Like an old yellow man?"

Ruby shook her head.

97

"Or a white man with him who does strange things?"

Ruby shook her head again. She noticed he stayed very close to the velvet-covered box. It was like an old wooden table model television set. She saw a few dials underneath one folded-back flap of the blue velvet. Corazon put his body between her and the box and Ruby knew that it was the secret weapon she'd been sent to find.

"Sweetheart, how you like to be rich?" Corazon said.

"No." Ruby shook her head. This whole job had more bad omens than a flock of ravens flying over a torture chamber. "Ever since I been a baby, I think money's just too much trouble. And what I need money for? With a big beautiful man like you, Generalissimo." Ruby smiled. She knew her smile did things to men, but it did nothing to this man.

"If you no help me now, you not my woman," said Corazon.

"I'll just have to deny myself." She fastened her belt and blew the dictator a kiss.

"It not hard. You go to yellow man and white man and give them two little pills when they drink. Then you come back to your lover, me. Eh? Great plan."

Ruby Jackson Gonzalez shook her head.

Corazon shrugged. "I charge you with treason. Guilty as charged. Go to jail."

This little indictment and trial over with, Ruby found herself being manhandled to a prison compound seventeen miles outside Ciudad Natividado on Baqian Route 1.

Meanwhile Corazon knew he had to do something about the two Americans without delay. He had broken relations with the United States, put himself in the hands of the Russians, and the Russians now claimed they had given forty-five lives to Baqia.

Which was true, but it only meant that forty-five Russians couldn't handle the two Americans.

And now the American woman wouldn't poison the pair and his own generals and ministers seemed to disappear, for fear they would be asked to attack the two devils in the Astarse Hotel.

The only one who was around was Major Estrada and Corazon did not want to use him. First, Estrada wasn't smart enough to do it and second, Corazon didn't want to lose the one man he knew who wouldn't kill him if he got a chance.

He thought briefly of going to the priest in the hills and throwing himself on his mercy. Maybe Juanita's prophecy could be made wrong. Maybe these Americans wouldn't team up with the holy man in the hills to overthrow Corazon?

He couldn't do it. It would loosen his grip on Baqia, and if that grip slipped he would be dead before the sun set. Show weakness and a dictator was finished.

There was only one thing to do. He had to make friends with America. This meant exposing himself to criticism from international organizations for human rights, which only recognized them for people who were friends of the United States. And it meant condemnation in the U.N. pickets in front of his three embassies in Paris, Washington, and Tijuana, and all sorts of general nuisance by people whose tails twitched when Moscow barked.

No matter. It would buy time. Make friends with America and maybe they would slow down whatever it was those two Americans planned to do. And that would give Corazon time to get into the hills and get rid of that holy man. And with him dead Juanita's prophecy could not come true.

Corazon sighed. He would do it.

He sighed again. Ruling a country was hard work.

CHAPTER SIX

The cable was marked "Top Secret Super Duper," so the secretary of state knew it was from Baqia when the thin blue sheet, folded into a self-envelope, was placed on his desk.

The message inside was from Generalissimo Corazon and was brief:

"We starting relations with you again, okay?"

The secretary of state chewed a Mylanta for his stomach, which bubbled like a noxious vial of chemicals from a horror movie. Nothing in the curriculum of the Woodrow Wilson School of International Affairs had prepared him for this. Why hadn't they told him about people like Corazon and governments like Baqia's?

They had broken off relations two days earlier by announcing that they weren't going to have sex with America anymore. No reason. Now they were re-opening diplomatic relations with a kindergarten note. Okay?

And it wasn't just Baqia, it was everywhere. Foreign policy seemed so easy when you were just lecturing about it. But when you tried to practice it you found the theories and the plans getting swamped by the people you had to deal with, people whose foreign policy might be dictated by whether or not they liked their morning meal.

And so the United States had lost its initiative in the Mideast, and every time they though they had put it back together that lunatic with a striped pillow case on his head would threaten to shoot somebody else and it would all come unglued. The United States had thrown its lot with the revolutionary rabble in South Africa and Rhodesia and, when the governments of those countries backed down with concessions, the revolutionaries rejected them. China seemed about ready to retreat back behind its traditional closed doors and no one knew who to talk to to try to prevent it.

And then there were natural resources. Was it some kind of cosmic joke of God to have the nitnats of the world breed and multiply over the oil and the gold and the diamonds and the chrome and the asphalt and now the mung?

He sighed again. Sometimes he wished that all the one-term talk of this President were true, so he could go back to college and lecture. At least a lecture was orderly, with a beginning, middle, and end. Foreign policy was nothing but middles.

He told his secretary to get Generalissimo Corazon on the telephone. If mung was that important, he would welcome El Presidente back into the American

102

family of nations, assuming El Presidente knew what the American family of nations was.

His secretary was back on the line in three minutes.

"They don't answer," she said.

"What do you mean they don't answer?"

"Sorry, sir. There's no answer."

"Well, get me the deputy El Presidente if they have one . . . or the minister of justice . . . or that dopey major that Corazon trusts. Yes, Estrada, I think it is. Get me him."

"He doesn't answer, either."

"He what?"

"I tried him. He doesn't answer, either."

"Is there anybody there I can talk to?"

"No sir, that's what I've been trying to tell you. The switchboard operator—"

"Where is she?"

"In Baqia."

"Of course she's in Baqia. Where in Baqia?"

"I don't know, Mister Secretary. They only have one operator in the whole country."

"What'd she say?"

"She said that the government had taken the day off. Call back tomorrow."

"The whole government? A day off?"

"Yes, sir."

The secretary of state popped another Mylanta.

"Okay," he said.

"Do you want me to try tomorrow, sir?" the woman asked.

"Not unless I tell you to. By then they may decide not to have sex with us anymore."

"I beg your pardon?"

"Forget it. Sorry."

So the secretary of state had no explanation of

Baqia's change of heart when he called the President of the United States to notify him that the relations were on again, okay?

"Why do you think they did it?" the President asked.

"Frankly, sir, I don't know. If I could find a way to take credit for it, I would. But I can't. Maybe the CIA pulled it off."

As luck would have it, the director of the CIA was in the White House, signing up for a new lawyers' insurance program. It was like Blue Cross and Blue Shield, but instead of paying for medical care it paid legal fees for government officials when they were indicted. Almost everybody on the White House staff and in the CIA had signed up.

The President asked to see the CIA director.

"The Baqians have opened relations with us again."

The CIA director tried not to show his surprise. All the personnel they had sent and had Ruby Gonzalez pulled it off? How? From jail? He had been advised by a friendly embassy of the fate of the CIA's last spy.

"That's good news. We were really making a major effort there," the director said. "I'm glad we got such quick results." He was thinking. Maybe Ruby Gonzalez did have something to do with it. There had been at least fifty foreign spies killed there since Ruby left the States. Maybe there was something, after all, to hiring minorities.

"According to my information, you had very minimal presence there," the President said. "That's what you finally agreed to, if you remember."

"That's not exactly how it worked out," said the director. "We sent a woman. We sent a black. We even had someone named Gonzalez. And I guess it all

104

worked out pretty well. The foreign bodies are piling up like garbage outside a French restaurant."

"Have you gotten reports from your agents?"

"Not yet," said the director.

"Where are they now?"

"I don't exactly know."

"What have they done while they've been in Baqia?"

"I don't exactly know," the director said desperately.

"You don't know what's going on there any more than I do, do you?" the President said.

"Actually, sir, I don't know exactly why Corazon decided to reinstate relations."

"Never mind. I do," the President said.

He dismissed the CIA director and went to the red telephone in the upstairs bedroom drawer. He lifted it off its base and the familiar voice of Dr. Harold W. Smith answered.

"Yes, sir."

"Congratulations. The Baqians have reopened relations with us."

"Yes," said Smith. "I was just informed."

The President was silent for a moment. He also had just been informed and the secretary of state only fifteen minutes earlier. How had Smith found out so fast? Did his sources extend right into the White House and the State Department? The President decided not to ask. He didn't want to know too much about how Smith worked.

"Do *you* know how it happened?" the President asked dryly.

"There have been forty-eight deaths of foreign agents in the last forty-eight hours," Smith said. "I would imagine our personnel had something to do with that. Did you send in CIA personnel?"

"Reluctantly, they agreed to send people," the President said.

"One of their agents is in jail, I am told," said Smith.

"Well, get him out. But primarily, we want that mung machine."

"The agent's a her," Smith said.

"Get *her* out, then. But the machine is really important. And, Doctor, I want to apologize for trying to call off your people earlier. I suspect they work differently from what I'm used to."

"They work differently from what everyone is used to, sir."

"Just tell them to keep at it."

"Yes, sir," said Smith.

Because the Baqian government had shut down for the day, the three telephone lines into the country were open and Smith had no trouble reaching Remo and Chiun in their hotel room.

Remo answered.

"This is Smith, Remo. How does it go on the—"

"Just a minute, Smitty. Is this business?"

"Of course it's business. Do you think I called to pass the time of day with you?"

"If it's business, talk to your man in charge. I'm retired, remember?" He held the phone out. "Chiun. It's Smith for you."

"I am here at the order of the President," Chiun said. "Why would I talk to underlings?"

Remo talked into the telephone again. "The President sent him here," he said. "Why should he talk to you?"

"Because I just talked to the President," Smith said.

Remo extended the telephone again. "He just talked to the President, Chiun."

Chiun rose from his lotus position as if he were levitating from the floor.

"This would not be a bad job," Chiun said. "If it were not for all these distractions."

"Suffer. It's your turn in the barrel now."

Chiun fixed his face in a broad smile before he spoke into the phone. He had learned that in a popular women's magazine as a way to appear vital and "with it" when speaking on the telephone. He did not know what "with it" meant, but he was sure vital was good.

"Hail, noble Emperor Smith. Greetings from the Master of Sinanju. The world trembles before your might and bows before your wisdom."

"Yes, yes," Smith said.

"I have not yet gotten to the good part," said Chiun. "Where the beasts of the field and the birds of the sky and yea, even the fishes of the sea rise up to proclaim their loyalty to you."

"Chiun, what's wrong with Remo?"

Chiun glanced carefully at Remo, who was sprawled on the bed, to see if anything about him had changed in the last few moments.

"Nothing," he said. "Nothing at all. He is the same as ever. Slothful, vile, indifferent to responsibility, uncaring about obligation, ungrateful."

Remo recognized the description. He waved a hand in acknowledgment.

"He is leaving this difficult assignment to me," Chiun said. "Because he is jealous that the President gave it to me directly, this responsibility to make the Baqians recognize our government as its friend."

"Well, you've done a good job on that."

"We do what we do," said Chiun, who did not know what Smith was talking about.

"Yes?" said Smith. "Just what is it you do?"

Chiun glanced at Remo and drew a series of circles around his temple with his right index finger.

"We make our presence felt," Chiun said. "But always as a mere reflection of your glory," he added quickly. "Yours and the real emperor's."

"Well, now the real part of the assignment remains," said Smith.

Chiun shook his head. That was the trouble with emperors. They were never satisfied. There was always something else to do.

"We stand ready to execute your orders," said Chiun.

"You stand ready," Remo called out. "I've quit."

"What did he say?" Smith asked.

"Nothing. He is just talking to himself. And since he cannot get an intelligent answer, he has taken to bothering us in our conversation."

"All right," Smith said. "The first and primary obligation is still the machine. We have to get it before anyone else does."

"We will do it."

"And there is an American agent in jail."

"And you want her killed?"

"No, no. She is in prison. Corazon put her there. We want her released."

"And you want the jailer killed? So he will take no such liberties again?"

"No, no. I don't want anybody killed. Just free this agent. Her name is Ruby Jackson Gonzalez."

"That is all?"

"Yes. Can you do it?"

108

"Before the setting of another sun," Chiun promised.

"Thank you."

"Such excellence of service is only your due, Emperor," Chiun said before hanging up. He told Remo, "I can't wait until my President decides to get rid of Smith. The man is a lunatic."

"*Your* President?" asked Remo.

"The House of Sinanju has a saying: 'Whose bread I eat, his song I sing.' My President."

"What does Smitty want you to do?"

"That machine again. Always everybody is worried about some machine. Now I ask you, how can they have an important machine in this country, which cannot even keep a hotel room clean?"

"You knew the machine was your assignment when you took this job," Remo said.

"And there is someone in jail whom Smith wants freed."

"How are you going to do that?" asked Remo.

"There is no way to do anything in this country. One cannot get clean towels or running water or decent food. I am going to the President, this Cortisone, and tell him what I want done."

"You think he'll listen to you? His name's Corazon."

"He will listen."

"When are you going?"

"The best time for the doing of a task is the moment of realizing the task exists. I am going now," Chiun said.

"I'm going with you," said Remo. "I haven't had a laugh all week."

Chiun went to the drapeless window of the room and as Remo watched he waved his arms and pointed

109

in elaborate gestures. He finally turned away with a satisfied nod.

"What was that all about?"

"The President, Corazon, was there. He looks in our window all day long. I told him I am coming."

"He's the President?" Remo asked. "I thought he was a Peeping Tom."

"He is Corazon."

"He's probably running like hell right now," said Remo.

"He will wait," Chiun said as he went to the door.

"What's the name of this agent you're supposed to get free?" Remo asked.

"Who knows? A woman. Ruby or something. I did not hear the rest. All American names sound alike."

CHAPTER SEVEN

Both the lieutenant of the guard and the sergeant of the guard had decided they were going to have their way with Ruby Gonzalez, rape being allowed when the prisoner involved was a political enemy, had offended the sainted person of El Presidente, and was good-looking enough to make the effort worthwhile.

Neither of them had scored because Ruby, out of the goodness of her heart, had warned each of them of the other's plan to put him out of the way—the sergeant wanting to do the lieutenant in so he could be promoted to the lieutenant's job, the lieutenant wanting to get rid of the sergeant so his undeserving brother-in-law could buy himself the sergeant's commission.

Ruby sat on the floor in her cell. There was a stuffed bag on legs that was supposed to be a mattress but she knew, without ever having been in jail that women prisoners who spent time lying or sitting on their beds asked for trouble.

Sooner or later, she knew, the sergeant or the lieutenant would be back with a gun for her. She had promised each of them that she would use the gun on his enemy, thus ensuring her benefactor's life and success. After the murder, she would be allowed to escape and no one would ever hear from her again and the Washington government would put $73 million in a Swiss bank account for the one who helped her.

The hardest part of the whole concoction had been deciding on the amount of money the U.S. would pay for her ransom. She figured she could probably get $5,000 out of the CIA. But thousands, she knew, wouldn't impress a Baqian. It sounded too much like hundreds. A million was right, but an even million sounded like a made-up number, like a fake. So she settled on $73 million. The seventy-three had the undeniable ring of truth, aided along by the fact that most Baqians couldn't calculate up to seventy-three.

It would work, she decided. Particularly since she had decided, from the time she met the first guard at the jail, that she could buy the entire Baqian civil service for the price of a three-pound can of decaffeinated coffee.

All she could do was wait for whichever guard was fool enough to give her a gun.

She didn't like waiting, doing nothing. So while she sat on the floor of the jail cell she began planning how she was going to expand her wig store. Financing would be no trouble. That problem had been resolved two years ago.

When she had first wanted to start her business, she had gone to the bank for a loan and the banker had laughed at her. The idea of a woman, twenty-one years old, black to boot, asking for a business loan without any collateral, well, it was just ridiculous and they weren't in the business of throwing away depositors' money, after all.

His high humor had lasted four hours after Ruby had left. Then the first pickets showed up in front of his bank, carrying signs advising black depositors that a new black-owned and operated bank was opening soon that would value their business and treat them like people. The sandwich boards they were carrying had a telephone number to call for information. The banker called the number.

Ruby answered.

The next day, she had her loan.

She had paid off the five-year note in two years, and her credit was now solid gold. She scratched numbers in the dust on the concrete floor of her cell. Twenty thousand dollars, that's what it would take to expand her buying system, so she had something more reliable than sailors carrying bags of smuggled hair. It would be easy.

They did not look like much. The American was skinny and had only thick wrists to indicate that he might have some power in his body. Corazon had thought the Oriental to be old. But he was more than old. He was aged and so frail that Corazon knew women from his mountain village who could fall on him and crush him.

But there was the evidence of the past two days. The dead British, the dead Russians. Corazon would be cautious.

"The people of Baqia welcome you visitors to our

beautiful island," he said. "We have always loved Americans."

Chiun waved away the small talk with a bony hand that protruded from the sleeve of his orange kimono.

Corazon would not be discouraged.

"If there is anything—"

"Towels," Chiun said. "Clean towels. Clean sheets. Anything else, Remo?"

"For openers, that's all right," Remo said.

"Done," said Corazon, although he could not understand why someone would want clean sheets and towels. "You will be happy to know that we have reinstituted the relations with your country."

Chiun turned to Remo. "What is he talking about?"

"Who knows?" Remo said.

"Does he think I'm an American?" asked Chiun.

"Probably. All you patriots look alike," Remo said.

"Generalissimo Corazon was talking about the bonds stronger than blood, the bonds of friendship and love that traditionally united Baqia and America.

"Enough," said Chiun. "We do not care about that. We care about towels and sheets."

Very strange, thought Corazon. "All right," he said. "Is there anything else?"

"That will do for now," said Chiun.

Remo pulled on the sleeve of his robe.

"Chiun, you forgot the woman. Ruby what's her name."

"And one thing more," Chiun told Corazon. "In one of your prisons, you have a woman."

"Lot of times, we have the woman in the prisons," said Corazon.

"This is an American woman named Ruby. She must be set free."

"You got it. Anything else?"

114

"Remo, anything else?"

"The machine, Chiun," Remo reminded him.

"And one thing more," said Chiun. "We want your machine. Our President said this was very important, to get your machine."

"Wonderful," Corazon said, beaming. His magic machine was kept at the prison under guard. To show his good will and his honesty and his loyalty to America and all the things it meant to him, he would meet Remo and Chiun at the prison. He would free the woman. And he would give them the machine. He was tired of it, anyway. He explained this loudly to an aide whom he ordered, "Get a car for these two wonderful Americans and do it quick or your ass be in the frying pan, boy."

"It be in front soon," Corazon told Remo and Chiun after the aide had left. He looked at the two men shrewdly.

"I like you two."

"It is allowed," Chiun said. Remo sniffed.

"You two pretty hot stuff, too," said Corazon. "You do some job on Russians and like that. I never saw anything like that."

Chiun nodded.

"I think now that I got relations again with the United States I gonna ask your President, let you two stay here. You help me train my men and they be best anticommunist fighters in all the Caribbean and those enslavers of the human mind never gain no foothold here in Baqia."

"We work only for the President of the United States," said Chiun. "Actually, this one . . ." He pointed to Remo. "He takes his orders from some underling, but I work directly for the President and it is

115

well-known that we of Sinanju find loyalty more important than mere wealth. So we must refuse your offer."

Corazon nodded sadly. He understood loyalty and morality and honesty. He had heard about them once.

Remo leaned toward Chiun. "Since when, Little Father? Since when all this loyalty to the United States? Since when have you stopped trying to promote side jobs?"

"Shhh," said Chiun. "I just told him that. There is no point in working for this one. He won't pay. I can tell. Look at the cheap furniture in this room."

The aide returned to announce, "The car is ready, Generalissimo."

Corazon rose from his gilt throne chair. "You two go ahead. The driver will know where to take you. I will meet you there, just to make sure that this Ruby is freed and that my men give you the machine, the way you want the machine. Because I want only the friendship and the relations between our countries."

Wordlessly, Chiun turned and walked toward the door. He said to Remo, "I don't trust this one."

"Neither do I," Remo said. "I've heard these love-America speeches before."

"I don't think we're ever going to get clean towels," said Chiun.

Corazon stood near the corner of the window, peering through the crack between the drape and the window frame. As soon as he saw Remo and Chiun's car pull away for the drive to the prison, he hollered for his aide to get his helicopter ready in the palace courtyard. Then he rolled the mung machine out from behind a curtain and toward the door to the elevator which would take it to the helicopter pad.

116

A half hour later, Remo and Chiun's car parked outside the open prison gates. They walked up to where Corazon stood by his helicopter.

"My men are getting the machine," he said. "The prisoner is in there." He pointed to a door in the corner of U-shaped central courtyard. "Here is the key to the cell."

Remo took the key. "I'll go get her," he told Chiun.

"I will go with you. For some reason, this Ruby person is important to my employer and so I want everything to go smoothly, to show them that if they give their assignments to someone who knows how to perform them competently, they will get satisfaction and full worth for their gold. That is the way of Sinanju."

"It's also the way of Sears Roebuck," Remo said testily. "Come along if you want to."

They went through the wooden door and were in a dark dank hallway. At the bottom of a flight of steps, a cell door, with bars set into it at eye level, faced them.

"I will wait here," said Chiun.

"You trust me to go down that flight of steps all by myself?" Remo asked.

"Just barely," Chiun said.

Inside her cell, Ruby Jackson Gonzalez tucked into her waistband the gun the sergeant of guards had given her. She heard the footsteps on the stairs. That would probably be the lieutenant on his way down for his promised assault on her.

When the sergeant had given her the gun, Ruby had told him what to do.

"Tell that lieutenant I wouldn't have any of you," she said. "Tell him like I got the hots for him."

"He never believe," the sergeant said. "He is a most

ugly man. How could he believe you reject me for him?

"Here," Ruby said. She flicked out a sharp index fingernail and dug a furrow down the sergeant's cheek. The little gap first filled up with blood and then a red trickle curled down his cheek.

The sergeant slapped his hand to his cheek. He looked at it when it came away red, then glared at Ruby.

"Bitch," he snarled.

He took a step toward her but Ruby smiled, a wide white smile that knew everything in the world.

"Hey, my honey," she said. "Now he believe you. That little scratch prove it. And when I get him, then you gonna be the lieutenant. New uniform, more money, you gonna be dashing. You have all the women you want. With that seventy-three million, you be *bad*."

He warmed to her smile.

"You, too?" he asked.

"I be the first and the best. And I see you messing with any other women, I take your head off," she said.

The smile wrung all the threat out of Ruby's words and forced a return smile from the guard.

"I bet you would," he said.

"You better bet," she said. "You too good-looking to let out loose." She stepped forward and blotted the guard's face with a handkerchief from his shirt pocket. She left a faint dried trail of blood on his cheek.

"There. Now you tell him and he believe you."

The sergeant nodded and left. Now Ruby heard the steps coming down the worn stone stairs. It should be the lieutenant but these didn't sound like the lieu-

118

tenant's feet. He wore heavy boots and liked to clomp around, trying to frighten people. But these footsteps were light and even, almost like a cat's pads.

She thought maybe the lieutenant already had taken his boots off, preparatory to spending the rest of the day in Ruby's bed.

"Sheeit," she said to herself.

She stood behind the door as the key opened it and the heavy door slowly swung open. She put her hand on the butt of the revolver, underneath her long white man-tailored shirt.

The door creaked to a stop. She heard a voice, distinctly an American's voice.

"Ruby?" the voice called.

It wasn't the lieutenant.

Ruby took her hand off the revolver and stepped out from behind the door. Her eyes met Remo's.

"Who you?" she asked.

"I've come to get you out."

"You from the CIA?" she asked.

"Well, something like that."

"Go 'way, dodo. You gonna mess me up around here," Ruby said.

"Hey, have I got the right place?" Remo said. "This is a jail and you're a prisoner and I've come to get you out."

"And if you from the CIA, you gonna mess everything up and we all get killed. If I get outa here on my own, I know I'm gonna get outa here. I let you take me outa here, I figure we all be shot before we goes twenty feet."

Remo reached over and chucked her under the chin.

"You're cute," he said.

"And you're country. Why you wearing them white socks with them black shoes?"

"I can't believe this is really happening," Remo said. "I come to rescue a woman from jail and she's bitching about the color of my socks."

"You couldn't rescue me from a tub of warm water," Ruby said. "Man don't care 'nough to dress right, don't know 'nough to do right."

"Hell with it. Stay," said Remo. "We'll go back in our jeep by ourselves."

Ruby shook her head. "Oh, I might as well go with you, make sure we gets out all right. How long you been gone from Newark?"

"Newark?" Remo said.

"Yeah. Say, you hard o' hearin' or you just dopey? Newark. It in New Jersey. How long you been gone from there?"

"How do you know that?"

"We all know how people talk in Newark 'cause we all gots relatives that lives there."

"I had expensive speech teachers help me get rid of my accent," Remo said.

"They took you, dodo. Get your money back."

"The government paid for it."

"No wonder," Ruby said. "Government always gets taken."

She was following Remo up the stone steps. Chiun stood inside the closed door, looking down at them.

"You think I dress funny, wait till you see this," Remo said to Ruby. "Chiun, you've finally met your match. This is Ruby."

Chiun looked at the young woman with disdain.

Ruby bowed to him, low from the waist.

"At least she knows how to greet someone," Chiun told Remo.

"Your robe is beautiful," she said. "What you pay for it?"

"This is a replacement of a very ancient robe that was unfortunately spoiled for me by a slug of a laundryman," Chiun said.

"Yeah, it was made in America. I see that. What you pay for it?"

"Remo," said Chiun. "The amount."

"I think it was two hundred dollars."

"You was taken," said Ruby. "They makes these robes in a little place near Valdosta, Georgia. I know the owner. He lots them out for forty dollars. So a hundred percent for wholesale and a hundred percent for retail and you shouldna paid no more than one-sixty."

"See, Remo, how you allowed us to be cheated again?" Chiun's voice was indignant.

"What do you care?" Remo said. "You didn't pay for it."

Ruby waved a hand at Chiun. "Listen up," she said. "Next time you needs a robe, talk to me. I get you something really good and the right price. Don't listen to this turkey no more. He wearin' white socks." She leaned close to Chiun and whispered. "He might be getting a rake-off for himself. Watch him."

Chiun nodded. "How true. Selfishness and greed are so often what one gets in return for dedication and love."

"Let's get out of here," Remo said in disgust. He moved toward the door behind Chiun.

"Wait, wait, wait, wait, wait," Ruby said, the words strung together so quickly that they sounded like a railroad conductor spitting out the name of a single lake in Wales.

"Who out there knows you in here?" she asked.

121

"Everybody," Remo said.

"Who everybody?"

"The warden. The guards. El Presidente himself," Remo said. "He came down to free you too."

"The big ugly dude with the medals?"

"Yeah. Generalissimo Corazon."

"You think he don' have no guns trained on this door right now?" Ruby asked.

"Why should he?"

"'Cause he a jerk. That man liable to do anything. Come on, we go upstairs and over the roof."

"We go out the front door," Remo said stubbornly.

Chiun put a hand on his arm. "Wait, Remo," he said. "There is wisdom in what this one speaks."

"You're just trying to con her into cutting the price of a robe," Remo said.

"Bunk it," Ruby said. "You go out the front door. The old gentlemans and I go upstairs. We mail your body wherever you want it sent."

She touched Chiun's elbow. "Come on. We go," she said.

Chiun allowed himself to be led up the stone steps. Remo watched them for a moment, glanced at the front door, then shook his head in disgust, and went up the steps, too. He slid by them to lead the way.

"Glad you finally coming around," Ruby said.

"If you want to walk with us, why don't you put that .38 you're carrying in the middle of your belt?" Remo said.

Ruby felt her shirt. The .38 was in the left side of her belt, covered by her long blouse.

"How you do that?" she said to Remo. "How you know I got a gun? How he do that?" she asked Chiun. Her voice rose into a coloratura squawk.

No one answered.

122

"You was looking and you saw the piece," Ruby said. She made it sound like an indictment for a capital crime.

"I didn't see it," Remo said.

"He didn't see it," Chiun agreed. "He hardly keeps his eyes open at all to see anything."

"How you do that?" Ruby insisted, her voice still a screech. "How you know it be a .38?"

This she had to know. Ruby saw instantly that there was real value in learning how to tell when someone was armed. She could copyright the method or patent it, if it was mechanical, then sell it to storekeepers in cities around America. They'd pay top dollar for a foolproof way of knowing that someone coming through their front door was carrying a gun.

"How you do that, I say?" she shrieked. Her voice, when she chose to use it that way, was high-pitched and abrasive. It sounded like it should be giving a locker-room critique to a high school football team losing 48–0 at half time.

"Anything if you stop screaming," Remo said. He was still leading the way up the steps. "You have the gun near your left hip. It throws off your balance when you walk. I can hear the heavier pressure on your left foot. The amount of pressure tells the weight of the gun. Yours weighs out as a .38."

"He really do that?" Ruby asked Chiun. "That dodo, he don't seem smart enough to do like that."

"Yes, that is what he did," Chiun said. "Sloppy, sloppy work."

"What?" asked Ruby.

"He did not tell you that your pistol has in it only three cartridges. If he were as alert as he should be, he would be able to tell that."

123

"He really did that? You really do that?" Ruby demanded.

"Yes," said Chiun.

"Pipe down," Remo told Ruby. "Your voice is like ice cubes cracking."

"How you learn to do that?" Ruby asked him.

"He taught me," Remo said.

"I taught him," Chiun said. "Of course, he does not learn as he should. Still, even a chipped pitcher is better than none at all."

"I want to learn how to do that," Ruby said. She was calculating. A half million storekeepers at a thousand dollars each. No, cut the price. Five hundred dollars each. Two hundred and fifty million dollars. Overseas rights. Around the world sales. Military application.

"I give you twenty percent of everything," she said to Chiun, softly so Remo would not hear.

"Forty percent," said Chiun who did not know what Ruby was talking about.

"Thirty," Ruby said. "I don' go no higher. And you take care of the turkey." She pointed at Remo.

"Done. A deal," said Chiun, who would have taken twenty percent if he knew what it was all about. He felt he had the better of it because he was stuck with taking care of Remo anyway.

"You got it," said Ruby, who would have given forty percent if she had to. "And no backing off now. We got a deal."

Remo pushed open the upstairs door. They were on a flat roof two stories about the central courtyard of the U-shaped compound.

They leaned over the edge and looked down where Generalissimo Corazon stood by his helicopter, a metal box in front of him. Corazon moved over to

124

squat behind the box, peering through a tube that served as a gunsight, aiming it at the door.

"Where are they?" Corazon grumbled to Major Estrada, who stood next to him, leaning against the plane, smoking.

"They'll be along," he said, smoking casually.

"See," hissed Ruby to Remo. "You go and you trustin' that big clown. He jiving you."

"All right, all right," Remo said. He leaned back and looked around the roof. There was a guard tower twenty yards away, rising ten feet above the roof, with a guard staring out at the Baqian countryside, his back to them.

"Wait here," Remo said. "Let me take care of that guard."

He moved slow and low across the top of the roof toward the guard's tower. At just that instant, the guard turned around. He saw Ruby and Chiun standing twenty yards away from him and Remo running toward him. He threw his rifle to his shoulder, drew a bead on Remo, and . . .

Boom. The guard's head exploded away as Ruby put a .38 slug between his eyes.

"You did not have to do that," Chiun clucked. "He could not have hit Remo."

"Don' matter to me none," Ruby said. "He coulda hit *me* if he'd a mind to. I'm watching out for number one." She smiled at Chiun, a warm afterthought. "Without me, your twenty percent goes down the tubes."

"Forty percent," corrected Chiun.

"Thirty," Ruby conceded. "But you take care of him."

Remo turned toward them in disgust as the guard

125

toppled over the low rail of the tower and fell heavily on the roof. His rifle clattered as it hit and bounced.

Remo ran back. "Let's get out of here."

In the courtyard below, Corazon saw them, poised on the roof, silhouetted against the almost white Baqian sky.

He grabbed the mung machine in his arms and wheeled around. With no attempt at deception, he pressed the firing button. The machine hummed for a split second and then there was a loud crackling noise.

His aim was off. The green glow of rays bathed the roof, but missed the three Americans. Instead they hit the door of the roof entrance, rebounded, and bathed the three in a dim glow.

Remo said, "We better . . ." His voice slowed down. "Go . . ." he tried to say, but the word would not come from his lips. He looked at Chiun, a surprised beseeching expression on his face, like a wordless cry for help. But Chiun's eyes already had rolled back into his head and his legs gave way under him and he fell to the roof. Remo collapsed on top of him.

Ruby had no time to wonder why the misaimed rays had toppled Remo and Chiun but had not harmed her. Time to think about it later. First things first. Number one. She moved to the far edge of the roof, ready to make the risky two-story jump down and start running. As she poised on the edge of the roof, she looked back. Remo and Chiun were lying together, looking like a pile of mixed laundry, Remo all cotton and Chiun all silk brocade.

She turned again to jump, then looked back once more.

She sighed and came away from the edge of the

roof. She picked up the guard's rifle as she raced back to Remo and Chiun.

"Sheeeit," she said. "I just knew that turkey'd muck everything up."

CHAPTER EIGHT

From down in the courtyard Corazon could not see that the first blast from the mung machine had felled Remo and Chiun. So he kept spraying the rooftop with bursts of energy from the device, but because the two men had fallen to the tarpaper roof the machine's rays passed harmlessly over them.

Still, Ruby Gonzalez wasn't going to take any chances.

She lay down on the roof to steady her aim, drew a careful bead on the mung machine, and fired her .38. The slug went wide and smashed a piece of metal out of a corner of the box.

"Damn borrowed gun," she spat. "No wonder this country don' amount to nothing."

She started to hoist the guard's rifle to her shoulder, but Corazon and Estrada already were hustling the mung machine back into the safety of the helicopter.

"Don't just stand there, fools," Corazon shouted to

troops and guards who hid under the first floor over-hang of the buildings. "Get up there. Capture them."

Corazon was hiding behind the helicopter when Ruby pinged a rifle shot into the soft side of the plane.

She glanced toward Remo and Chiun.

"C'mon, you two. Get up," she said. "C'mon now. Get yo' butts movin'."

They lay still and unmoving.

Ruby fired two more rifle shots to slow down the troops who were clambering up the steps leading to the rooftop that faced hers from across the courtyard. The position was desperate.

If Remo and Chiun couldn't move, she could not hold out much longer. She couldn't do much damage with borrowed guns, but if she kept firing and forced the soldiers to take her with overwhelming firepower, it was probable that the white man and the Oriental would be killed by stray bullets.

The soldiers were now on the rooftop across from her and had begun laying down a line of bullets.

"We all gets dead and nobody saves nobody," Ruby said to herself. She leaned over to Chiun and spoke into his ear, hoping he might hear her. "I be back for you," she said. "I be back."

She rolled away from the two men so they would be less likely to get hit by soldiers returning her fire. She fired two more shots from the rifle. Every time she fired, she noticed all the soldiers ducked their heads.

She moved back toward the wall leading to the countryside surrounding the prison compound. As she neared the edge she fired two more shots and then shouted at the top of her voice.

"Stop firing! We surrender!"

130

Before the soldiers could look up from their hiding places, Ruby jumped off the roof, twenty feet to the ground below.

The soldiers waited on the opposite roof for further evidence of the surrender.

Corazon's bellowing voice filled the now-silent compound.

"They said they surrender, you idiots. Get over there and get them." He carefully remained hidden behind the helicopter.

Reluctantly, the soldiers began to move, afraid of a sneak attack by the one woman arrayed against them.

When no bullets were fired, the bravest of them stood up. He was not shot down so all the rest stood and began to run to the other side of the roof.

When they got there, they found Chiun and Remo lying unconscious on the roof. Ruby was gone.

"The lady be gone," a sergeant shouted to Corazon. He wondered if her successful escape, even though not quite as planned, still entitled him to $73 million. "But the two men be here."

"Bring them down," Corazon said. "And search for her."

The soldiers looked over the edge of the wall at the land outside the prison compound.

The terrain stretched away flat and empty for miles in all directions. The woman could have found no shelter in that barren landscape. Running, she would have been picked out as easily as an ink blot on a marshmallow. The soldiers scanned in every direction.

Ruby Gonzalez had vanished.

The soldiers dumped the bodies of Remo and Chiun in the dirt in front of Corazon.

"They been shot?" he asked.

The soldiers shook their heads.

Corazon cackled. "So they got more power than me, eh? Cousin Juanita, she say so, eh? More power than me? Here's their power, laying in the dirt."

He kicked Remo in the side with his right foot and smashed out at Chiun's belly with his left foot.

"We see now who has the power." Corazon looked at the soldiers around him. "Who is the all-powerful?" he demanded.

"El Presidente, Generalissimo Corazon," they shouted in unison.

"That's right," he said. "Me. The power."

He looked down at the two unconscious men.

"What you want down with them, Generalissimo?" Major Estrada asked.

"I want them put in cages. Put them in cages and then drive them back to my palace. I want them at my palace. Got it?"

Estrada nodded. He pointed to a lieutenant of the guards and told him to take care of it.

Corazon stepped toward the helicopter.

"You going back to the palace?" Estrada asked.

"Sure thing," said Corazon. "I got to break off the relations with the United States." He chuckled as he clambered onto the helicopter. "The power. I the power. Me."

He did not hear the voodoo drums begin thumping again in the nearby hills.

CHAPTER NINE

Route 1 back to Ciudad Natividado was pitted and broken and the jeep bumped up and down off the roadway as its driver moved along. Although Baqia produced 29 percent of the world's asphalt through giant pitch lakes that dotted the island, it apparently never occurred to anyone in government to use the asphalt to pave the roadway.

In the back of the jeep, the bodies of Remo and Chiun were jammed into two small iron cages barely three feet high by two feet wide and deep. Guards sat on the back of the vehicle, their eyes scanning the barren countryside as if expecting an attack on foot any moment from Ruby Gonzalez.

And underneath the jeep Ruby Gonzalez kept her right arm hooked around the rifle she had jammed up into the vehicle's chassis and her legs over the jeep's frame.

Rocks from the pitted road kicked up and abraded

her back, but she had been careful to get on the side away from the muffler, so she would not be burned by the heat. She figured she was good for forty-five minutes under the jeep before she couldn't hang on anymore. If that happened, she planned to release her rifle, slide out from under the jeep, blow out a tire with her first shot and hope to catch the three soldiers with her next shots before they got her. Risky, she thought, but better than nothing. Best of all, though, would be getting back to Ciudad Natividado.

Thirty minutes after leaving the prison compound, she could tell they had entered the capital city by the increase in people noise. When the jeep stopped for something, Ruby could hear voices crowding near. They were speaking island Spanish and talking about Remo and Chiun.

Ruby quietly let herself down into the dirt roadway under the jeep and lay there. As soon as the jeep pulled away and its wheels passed on either side of her, she scrambled to her feet and took a step into the crowd of people.

"Only way to get ride from de soldiers, okay?" she said in a passable imitation of the island's Spanish. Before anyone could answer she had walked away and headed for the outdoor peddlers' stalls.

The chances were that the Baqian soldiers would not remember to put a guard on her room to catch her if she came back, but she couldn't afford to take the chance.

The presidential helicopter already had landed inside the palace compound and Corazon was in his reception room talking to Estrada.

"Machine worked good on them," he said.

"They alive," Major Estrada pointed out.

134

"Yeah, but I not hit them square. It was a wing shot," Corazon said.

"When you knock them out, why you not melt them then? When you got them close?"

"That's why I president for life and you never be," Corazon said. "First I keep them alive and the United States got to be careful how it deals with me. Maybe I parade these two into a war crimes trial and mess up America if they give me any more trouble."

"As long as they alive, you got trouble. Remember what you cousin Juanita she say."

"She say some power gonna give me trouble with the holy man from the mountains. But I gonna take care of that a different way."

"What different way?"

"I gonna go to the mountains and do what I shoulda do a long time ago. I gonna get rid of that old man. I the president for life, I should be the leader of the religion, too."

"No president ever did that before," Estrada cautioned.

"No president ever as glorious as Generalissimo Corazon," the president said modestly.

"Hokay," said Estrada. "So what's you want to do?"

"I want you to put those cages in the middle of the town. Put guards around them. Put a sign on them that this is how Baqia treats CIA troublemakers. Then you drop everything else and go call the United States and tell them we breaking off the relations."

"Again? I did that yesterday."

"And I undid it today. You go do it."

"Why we do that, General?"

"Generalissimo," said Corazon.

"Right, Generalissimo. Why we do that?" Estrada asked.

"Because we better off dealing with Russians. If I breaks with America, they yell a lot but they leave me alone. If I stays break with Russia, they send somebody to kill me. That's no fun. And it better to be communist. Nobody start yelling at us for having political prisons and no food for the peasants and like that. Only countries that line up with America has to feed people. Look at the Arabs. They got all that money but they don't pay for nothing in the United Nations. Only American allies got to pay."

"Shrewd, Generalissimo," said Estrada. "That all you want me to do?"

"No. When you gets that all done, get the limousine ready. We gonna go out into the mountains and we gonna get that old man and kill him dead."

"People not like that, killing the religious leader."

"People not know anything about it," Corazon said. "Stop worrying. Now I gotta go take a nap and when I wake up, then we go. Any new women around?"

"I haven't seen any."

"Okay, I go to sleep by myself. Go put them cages in the square. And don't forget the guards."

Ruby Gonzalez traded her trousers and shirt, even up, for a Caribbean-style mumu, a long shapeless flowered green gown. But the belt wasn't part of the deal, she insisted.

When the woman in the peddler's stall agreed, Ruby went in the back of the stall, put on the gown, and underneath it took off her other clothes. She buckled her trousers belt around her bare waist. It would be handy to jam a gun into if she could get to her room to get a gun.

Then she sat on the dirt floor, out of sight of anyone on the street, and began running her fingers through her Afro, pulling it straight up from her head. When she had finished, the pure circular outline of the Afro was gone. Hair stuck up in clumps, straight away from her head, as if she were continuously being jolted with electricity.

Then, with practiced fingers, she parted her hair into sections and began braiding it into tight neat rows that lay close to her head. It took her five minutes. When she was done, she stood up and gave her trousers and shirt to the peddler.

With the corn rows and the shapeless dress, Ruby looked enough like a native Baqian to pass. She would have had to smile that wide, even smile for someone to have suspected otherwise, because her teeth were white and perfect and no one else on the island that she had yet seen had a halfway decent mouth of teeth. No problem, she realized. Not much to smile about.

While she had worked on her hair, Ruby had been thinking. The white dodo and the old Oriental had come to free her. But she had not been in prison long enough for them to have been sent from the States on that mission. They must have been in Baqia already and had gotten the assignment while there. How? The most logical way was by telephone, although she knew the CIA was so lunatic sometimes that they might have used skywriters to send their secret agents their secret assignments.

The telephone, most likely. It was worth a chance.

She found the headquarters, field office, maintenance division, installation unit, and operations center of the ding-a-ling National Baqian Supreme Telephone Network in a one-story cinder-block building at the end of the capital city's main street. The person on duty was the director, maintenance chief, installation coordinator, customer service representative, and operations officer. That meant it was her turn to run the switchboard.

She was sleeping when Ruby went inside because Baqia's three outside telephones didn't get much business, so Ruby of course told her she understood how hard the woman worked and how little the government appreciated her efforts to make Baqia a leader in international communication and sure, wasn't it just a few hours ago that her boyfriend had told her how quick he had gotten a telephone call from his boss in the States, but he had lost his boss's phone number and where did that telephone call come from anyway? And Ruby wouldn't even ask except she knew that this woman would know everything about telephones and that's what she told her boyfriend—Ruby glanced at the nameplate on the desk—she told her boyfriend that Mrs. Colon would know anything and everything about the telephones because in Baqia everybody knew that Mrs. Colon was what kept the country running and what was that number again? And the name of the boss? And I bet you could just get that nice Doctor Smith on the telephone again real fast so I can give him my boyfriend's message, because if Mrs. Colon couldn't do it, it couldn't be done.

When Mrs. Colon got Dr. Smith back on the line, Ruby worried for a moment about her overhearing the conversation but the worry was unfounded. The operator went right back to sleep.

"Listen, you Doctor Smith?"

"Yes."

"Well, they got your two men. They hurt."

"My two men? What are you talking about?"

"Look, don't jive me. I don't have a lot of time."

138

Smith thought a moment. "Are they hurt badly?"

"I don't know. I don't think so. But don't worry about it. Anyway, I'm gonna take care of it."

"You? Who are you?"

"You and I have the same uncle," Ruby said. "The big guy in the striped pants."

"And the machine?" Smith said. "That's what's most important."

"Even more than your men?" asked Ruby.

"The machine is the mission," Smith said coldly. "Nothing is more important than that mission."

Smith had barely hung up when the red panic telephone rang inside the top left drawer of his desk.

"Yes, Mister President."

"What the hell is going on now? That lunatic Corazon has just broken relations with us again. What are your men doing, anyway?"

"They've been captured, sir," said Smith.

"Oh, my God," the President said.

"I was told not to worry," Smith said.

"Who told you *that* stupid thing?" the President snarled.

"Ruby Jackson Gonzalez."

"And who the hell is Ruby Jackson Gonzalez?"

"I think she works for you, Mister President," Smith said.

The President was silent a moment. He was remembering the CIA's "big effort" in Baqia. A woman. A black. Spanish-speaking. One Goddam person. Just one. He'd fix that CIA director's ass.

"She say anything else?" the President asked.

"Just one comment," Smith said.

"Which was?"

"It's not really germane to our problem, sir," Smith said.

139

"Let me be the judge of that," the President said. "What'd she say?"

"She said that I be one mean mother to work for," Smith said.

The afternoon sun was like a hammer pounding at his skull and Remo groaned as he came to. His body felt cramped, as if he had been tied in a knot, and it took him a moment to realize where he was. He was in some kind of cage; the buzzing around him was the sound of people talking. He squinted and opened his eyes. There were faces staring at him on all sides. People jabbering at him in Spanish. *Mira. Mira.* They were calling their friends. Look. Look. *Mira. Mira.*

They had caged him and he was in the city square of Ciudad Natividado. But where was Chiun?

Remo opened his eyes wide. It felt as if they had been glued shut and it took all his strength just to open them. There was another cage next to him and Chiun was in it. He was lying on his side, his face toward Remo and his eyes open.

"Chiun, are you all right?" Remo gasped.

"Speak Korean," Chiun said.

"I guess we've been captured," Remo said in his thin Korean.

"You are very perceptive."

Chiun was all right, still alive enough to be nasty.

"What was it?" Remo said.

"Apparently the machine with the rays."

"I didn't think he could hit us with it," Remo said.

"Probably he did not. But we were told it does not work well on drunks. It works best on those with well-developed nervous systems, whose senses all work. And since ours work so much better than anyone else's, just deflected rays from the machine rendered us this way."

A young boy slipped by the guard who stood in front of their cages and poked at Remo with a stick. Remo tried to grab it out of the child's hand, but the little boy easily pulled it away. Remo clenched his fist and he could not feel tension build up in his forearm. He was awake but without strength, without even the strength of an average man.

The child started to poke again with the stick, but the guard slapped the side of the child's head and the young boy ran away crying.

Remo looked to his other side for another cage. There was none.

"Where's Ruby?" he asked Chiun.

A woman's voice came from near his ear, softly. "Here's Ruby, dodo."

Remo turned to look into the face of a woman with corn rows and a native dress. Only by her smile was he sure it was Ruby Gonzalez.

He looked at her native dress again.

"Now that's *real* country," he said. "Don't ever grouse about my white socks again."

"I spoke to your boss, Doctor Smith," she said.

"You did? How'd you get to him?"

"Don't worry about it. He one mean bastard."

"That was him," Remo said.

"Anyways, I got to go after the machine first. But then I be back for you. You all right?"

"No strength," Remo said. "The strength's been drained."

Ruby shook her head. "I knew you was going to be trouble when I first saw you. I just knew it."

"Listen, just get us out of here."

"I can't do it now. Too many people. The head man

141

here, he just went off in his limousine with his machine. I'm gonna follow him. I'll try to get you loose tonight. Meanwhile, you rest up, try to get some strength back. Trust yo Aunt Ruby."

"If it wasn't for you, we wouldn't be here," Remo said.

"If it wasn't for me stopping you from going out that door at the jail, you'd be a puddle. I be back." Ruby saw the guard turn to look at her and she twisted her face into a mask of hatred and rage and began screaming at Remo in Spanish. *"Yankee dog, Beast. Killer spy."*

"All right, you," the guard said. "Get outa there."

Ruby winked at Remo and drifted off into the crowd, which was still pointing and jeering. Remo looked at the faces twisted in hatred at him and to close them out he shut his eyes and drifted back to sleep.

He was not afraid for himself, but he was overcome with a feeling of shame that Chiun, the Master of Sinanju, should be subjected to this humiliation. The thought filled him with an intense fury, but he could not feel the fury fill his muscles with strength.

Revenge would have to wait until later, he thought. At least until he woke up.

But that was all right. Revenge was a dish best served cold.

CHAPTER TEN

Following Corazon was easy for Ruby after she stole the army jeep.

She just followed the sound of the gunshots, because Corazon considered himself a hunter and while he was being driven pegged shots through the window of his limousine at everything that was not rooted. And sometimes rooted.

He shot at deers, at squirrels, at jungle rats and lizards, at cats and dogs, and when he did not see any of those he shot at trees, bushes, and, as a last resort, grass.

Major Estrada, sitting in the back seat next to him, refilled the general's gun when it was necessary.

"I get rid this old guy," said Corazon, "and then I boss of everything." He blinked a shot at a stump, which he thought had blinked at him. "No more worry about the voodoo people in the hills. No more

143

worry about the holy man leading a revolution. This take care of it all."

"Sounds good to me," said Estrada. He took the pistol from the general and refilled it from a box of shells he carried on the back shelf ot the Mercedes limousine.

Corazon pressed the electric button to roll up the back window as the sky darkened quickly and a flash thunderstorm hit. It was one of the byproducts of the tropical breezes and the warm, humid weather. Every day there were more than a dozen thunderstorms, never lasting more than a few minutes, barely dropping enough rain to dampen the dust of the island.

Five minutes later, Corazon depressed the switch again and lowered the window. The sun was shining brightly.

They drove another twenty-five minutes before the driver stopped at the base of a small mountain. A narrow footpath curled its way around the side of the hill. It was not wide enough for a vehicle.

The nose of the car was stopped at a slick black lake of goo, extending eighty yards long by twenty yards across.

Corazon stepped from the car and looked at the oily pool.

"If nature had give us oil instead of tar, we would be wealthy men. A wealthy country," he said.

Estrada nodded.

"Still, tar is all right," Corazon said. He plunked a pebble onto the lake of pitch. It sat atop the shimmery surface, floating there. "Tar all right. None of us starve," the Generalissimo said.

He looked to the two soldiers in the front seat. "Come on along with that machine," he said. "And be careful. We gonna use it soon."

144

He laughed a rich big belly laugh as he walked off, the three soldiers following him onto a small path that skirted the tar pit and led to the walk up the mountainside.

The four men were just skirting the pitch lake when Ruby Gonzalez' jeep pulled up behind the limousine. She saw them walking away, the two soldiers lugging the heavy mung machine, and she could see their destination was the small cluster of huts at the top of the hill. The sounds of drums resonated in the air, gently, as if from far away.

Ruby backed up her jeep and drove it into thick brush where it could not be seen from the road.

She got out of the vehicle and looked up at the broad back of Corazon, slowly moving up the mountain. He was followed by Estrada and the two soldiers carrying the machine. As she looked the sun moved from behind a cloud and shone down brightly on the black lake of pitch, and at that moment Corazon, Estrada, the two soldiers, the entire mountain seemed to shift in Ruby's vision, as if it had all moved twenty yards to the left. She blinked her eyes, not believing what she saw. She opened them again. The images she was watching were still displaced.

She realized she was seeing a mirage. The bright sun was shimmering on the rain water on the surface of the tar pit and the vapors acted like a giant prism, moving images from where they should be.

She filed the phenomenon away as incidental information, then pushed her way through the brush and overgrowth and around the left side of the tar pit and began to clamber up the hill.

Her direct path was rougher, but would get her to the village before Corazon and his men.

As she neared the crest of the small mountain and the grass huts there, the sound of the drums grew louder.

There were a half-dozen huts, built in a semicircle around a pit in which logs burned, despite the blistering heat of the Baqian summer. The drums which Ruby thought might come from the village were still sounding, from even farther away.

There was a sweet flower smell in the air, the scent of cheap after-shave.

As Ruby pushed onto the crest of the hill, she felt a strong pair of arms encircle her from behind. She looked down. They were bare black arms, a man's.

"I want to talk to the old man," she said in island Spanish. "Hurry, fool."

"Who are you?" a voice asked. It was a voice that sounded as if it had been rebounding around the walls of a tunnel for six weeks before reaching someone's ears.

"Some people are coming here to kill him and you, fool, stand here with your arms caressing my breasts. Quickly. Take me to him. Or are you afraid of a woman who carries no weapons?"

Another voice bit the air.

"A woman without weapons would be a strange woman indeed." She looked across the clearing. A small, wizened man with skin the color of roasted chestnuts was walking toward her. He wore black cotton trousers with ragged bottoms and no shirt. Ruby guessed his age at seventy.

He nodded as he reached them and the arms came loose from around Ruby. She bowed to the man and kissed his hand. She knew nothing of voodoo, but marks of courtesy were marks of courtesy everyplace.

"Now what is this about someone coming to kill me?" the man asked. Behind him, Ruby saw people peering from behind the grass huts.

"Corazon and his men. They are on the hillside now. He wants to kill you because he fears you threaten his rule."

Without taking his eyes from Ruby's, the old man snapped his fingers. Behind him a young woman ran from behind one of the huts over to the edge of the clearing, looking down on the path below.

She scurried back to the old man.

"They come, master. Four of them. They carry a box."

"Corazon's new weapon," said Ruby. "It kills."

"I have heard of this new weapon," the old man said. He looked at the man behind Ruby and nodded. "All right, Edved. You know what to do."

The man brushed by Ruby and walked away. She saw he was a giant of a black man, almost seven feet tall, skin glistening plum-colored in the hot afternoon sun.

"My son," the old man said.

"Most impressive," Ruby said.

The old man took her elbow and led her to the other side of the small plateau.

"I guess it would not be good for the Generalissimo to find you here?" he said.

"No, it wouldn't."

"An American?" he asked as he led Ruby down the hillside, away from Corazon's men.

"Yes."

"I thought so. But you speak the island language well. And your costume would fool almost anyone."

Forty feet down the hillside, the old man stopped

147

on a flat outcropping of rock. He pushed aside heavy brush and vines that grew from a tree and Ruby saw the opening to a cave. The cool air from inside felt like full-blast air conditioning.

"Come. We will be safe here and we can talk," he said.

He led her inside and as the vines closed, they muffled the sound of the distant drums, beating their insistent forty beats a minute, and she realized that she had become so accustomed to their sound that she no longer heard them.

The old man squatted on the ground in the dark cave, managing somehow to look regal in that inelegant posture.

"My name is Samedi," he said.

The name hit Ruby like a sudden attack of migraine.

She was five years old again and visiting her grandmother in Alabama. And one evening she wandered away from the shabby little house near the fly-buzzing pond and down the road and found herself outside a cemetery.

Night was falling fast, but she saw people inside the cemetery and she leaned on the stone wall to watch, because they were dancing and they seemed to be having a good time. Ruby started dancing, too, where she was standing, wishing she was grown so she could go over and dance with the big people. And then their dance stopped and a man with no shirt but wearing an Abraham Lincoln stovepipe hat came out of the far darkness, and the dancers fell to the ground and began to chant.

It was hard for Ruby to make out what they were saying because she had never heard the word before, but she listened carefully, and she recognized it. They were saying:

"Samedi. Samedi. Samedi."

Suddenly, Ruby didn't feel like dancing anymore. A chill swept her body, a sense of nameless fear, and she remembered she was five years old and this was a graveyard and it was night and she was far from home, and she bolted and ran back to her grandmother.

The old woman comforted the frightened child in her big warm arms.

"What happened, child?" she asked. "What give you this fright?"

"What is Samedi, Granna?"

She felt the old woman stiffen.

"You was down de cemetery?" the old woman said.

Ruby nodded.

"Some things child just don' gotta know about, 'ceppin' you stays 'way from de graveyard at night," her grandmother said.

She squeezed Ruby hard to her, as if to accentuate her order, and Ruby stayed there, feeling warm and loved and protected, but still wondering, and later when her grandmother tucked her into bed, she asked again.

"Granna, please tell me, what is Samedi?"

"All right, chile, 'cause I get no rest iffen I don' answer you. Samedi be the leader of them people you saw dancin' down there."

"Then why was I ascared?"

"Because those people not like us. Not like you and me."

"Why aren't they like us, Granna?" Ruby asked.

Her grandmother sighed in exasperation. "Because they be already dead. Now hush your face and go to sleep." And the next day her grandmother would not speak about it anymore.

Ruby's mind was back in the cave and the old man Samedi was talking to her.

"Why would Corazon be here to kill me?" he asked.

"I don't know," said Ruby. "There are two Americans in town and he thinks that they're here to make you the ruler of this country."

"These Americans, they are with you?"

"No. We came separately to Baqia. They are now captives, so I am responsible for them. Corazon must want you dead so they will have no chance of succeeding in making you ruler."

The old man looked at Ruby with coal black eyes that sparkled even in the faint light of the cave.

"I don't think so," he said. "The government is Corazon's. The religious life is mine. It has always been that way and these mountains are far from Ciudad Natividado."

"But you thought enough of what I said to come to this cave with me to avoid Corazon," Ruby said. "You did not do that because you trust him as a brother."

"No. One must never trust Corazon too much. He killed his own father to become president. If he were to be leader of the island's religion he would rule for life. No one could oppose him."

"He has the army. Why hasn't he come for you before then?"

"The people of the island would not tolerate an attack on a holy man," Samedi said.

"But if they never knew? If you were one day just to vanish from the earth and Corazon made himself religious leader, he would be invincible. And as sure

150

as God made green apples, he would lead Baqia into disaster and maybe war."

"You overstate it," Samedi said. "He is not a good man. He is not to be trusted. But he is not the devil."

"He *is* the devil," said Ruby. "And that is why I want you to help me overthrow him."

Samedi thought for only a few seconds before shaking his head no. Over the very faint thump of distant drums, there were suddenly women's screams to be heard, drifting down from the mesa above their heads.

Samedi cocked his head toward the sound, then looked back at Ruby.

"Corazon is asking where I am," he said. "But they will not speak. The only words spoken in these hills are the words of the drums and they speak all words to all men. No. As long as Corazon does not attack me, I will not attack him."

They sat in silence. There was a sharp crack and another set of women's screams and then all was silence except for the faraway thumping and bumping of the drums, like slow lazy rubber hammers attacking the skull.

They continued sitting in silence until they heard a woman's voice. "Master, Master! Come quickly."

Samedi led Ruby out onto the hillside, then strode quickly up the hill to the grass huts. A woman waited for him at the top of the hill. Tears rolled down her black face, like glycerine drops on chocolate pudding.

"O Master! Master," she sobbed.

"Be strong now," he said, pressing her shoulder. "The general is gone?"

"Yes, Master, but . . ."

Samedi had walked away from her. He stood in the

151

center of the village, among men and women who were looking down at the ground where there was a greenish black oily slick.

Ruby pushed through the people and stood at his side.

Samedi looked around at all the faces. They were weeping quietly.

"Where is Edved?" he asked.

The silent weeping turned to sobbing and screams of anguish.

"Master, Master," one woman said. She pointed down at the green slick on the dry dusty dirt of the hilltop.

"Enough weeping. Where is Edved?"

"There," she said. She pointed at the slick of green. "There is Edved," and she let out a shriek that would curdle milk.

Samedi sank slowly to his knees and looked at the bile on the ground. He extended his hand as if to touch it, then withdrew it.

He knelt there for long minutes. When he rose and turned to Ruby there were tears in the corners of his eyes.

"Corazon has declared a war," he said slowly. "What is it you want me to do? I will do anything."

Ruby could not take her eyes off the green slick on the ground. The thought that somehow Corazon had reduced that giant young man to nothing more than a memory and a puddle made her shudder with loathing.

She looked into Samedi's eyes.

"Anything you want," he repeated.

And then he clapped his hands. Once. The sound reverberated like a pistol shot over the tiny village and carried out into the bright afternoon air, like an order.

And the drums stopped.

And the hills and the mountains were silent.

CHAPTER ELEVEN

There were no streetlights in Ciudad Natividado.

The city square was pitchblack and still except for the throbbing in Remo's temple.

But it wasn't throbbing. He was awake now and he realized the throbbing came from outside himself. It was the drums and they were louder than he had heard them before. Closer.

He lay quietly in his cage, feeling the cool of the Baqian night. He could sense that the guards standing alongside the cages were edgy. They shuffled back and forth from foot to foot and they spun around nervously, looking behind them, every time a night animal cried.

And the drums *were* getting louder, growing in intensity.

Trying to make no sound, Remo slowly extended his fingers toward the nearest bar of his cage.

His fingers circled the inch-thick metal. He

squeezed, but felt no give of metal under his hand. He was still without strength. His body ached from the cramped position he had slept in.

He turned quietly in his cage, moving his head around to see how Chiun was.

His face was near the bars on the side of Chiun's cage. Through the bars he saw Chiun's face. The Oriental's eyes were open. His finger was at his mouth and he gave Remo a shushing gesture to keep him quiet.

They lay still and listened to the drums grow louder.

Louder and closer, louder and closer the distant thumping which had hung over the island like weather now was taking on a physical reality by its changing.

And then the drums stopped. The air was heavy with stillness.

And then there was another sound, a scratch as if something were being dragged across gravel. Remo listened intently. His muscles were weak but his senses seemed to be coming back. It was someone walking, scuffing his feet in the gravel and dirt. No. Two people walking.

And then Remo saw them.

Two men. Fifty yards away, at the end of the main street of Ciudad Natividado. They were shirtless and wore white trousers. Even in the dim moonlight and the occasional beam of light through a window of the presidential palace, Remo could see their eyes, bugged, large whites, staring out of their heads.

They were scuffing forward now, their feet kicking up small swirls of dust in the dry street.

They were only twenty-five yards away when the guards spun and saw them.

"Stop!" one guard shouted.

The two men kept coming on, slowly, like glaciers inexorably powerful, and they lifted their hands in front of them as if they were divers approaching the edge of the high board. They opened their mouths and a thin low wail came forth. And the drums started again, so close that it seemed to Remo that their distance must be measured in feet now, not miles.

One of the guards shouted, "Stop or we'll shoot!"

The moan from the two men grew higher in pitch, climbing the scale of sound until it was a bitter high wailing scream.

The guards waited, looked at each other, then screamed themselves as the two men came clearly into sight.

"*Duppy!*" screamed one.

"Zombie!" shouted the other.

They dropped their rifles and ran toward the presidential palace.

Now Remo heard footsteps running quickly in the dirt street and then he felt his cage being lifted into the air and he was being carried away. When he looked back, the two men in white trousers had turned and were shuffling back the way they had come, their scuffing feet still kicking up dust in the street, but silent now, their wailing ended. Then they vanished into the dark at the end of the street.

Remo looked up to see who was carrying his cage but he saw only black faces against a blacker night.

They were carried into a small wooden shack. Its interior was dimly lit with candles and the windows were sealed with tar paper to prevent any light from spilling outside.

Remo looked up. Four black men had been carrying him and Chiun. Wordlessly they went to work on

157

the cage padlocks with heavy bolt-cutters. Two strong snips and the cages were open. Remo crawled out, then stood up on the dirt floor. He stretched his muscles and almost fell to the ground. Chiun was standing alongside him and he put a hand onto Remo's arm for support.

The four black men glided toward the door and were gone.

Remo turned to look at them, to thank them, but before he could speak he heard a familiar voice.

He turned around to see Ruby staring at him, wearing a green tentlike dress, her hair neatly arranged in corn rows. She was staring at him, shaking her head.

"Minute I see you," she said, "I know you gonna be nothin' but trouble, dodo."

"You're cute, Ruby," Remo said.

He reached forward to touch her, lost his balance, and fell forward. Ruby caught him in her arms.

"I don' know what you get paid," she said as she struggled him over to a cot on the floor, "and I don' wanna know, 'cause it gonna be more than I make and I gonna be sick, 'cause anythin' they pay you's too much. Lay down and let Ruby fix you up."

She arranged Remo on the cot, then helped Chiun to the other cot in the room.

"I gonna get some food in you. Both you too skinny."

"We don't eat most things," Remo said. "We have a special diet."

"You eat what I gives you," said Ruby. "You think this some fancy white man's hotel? I gotta get you fixed up so we can take care of the general and get us outa here in one piece."

"And just how do you propose to do that?" asked Remo. "Corazon's got the machine and the army."

158

"Yeah, fish, but there something he ain't got."

"What's that?" asked Remo.

"Me," Ruby said.

She went to Chiun and pulled a thin clean sheet up over him.

"Why do you call Remo fish?" asked Chiun.

"He look like a fish," she said. "He got no lips at all."

"He can't help that," Chiun said. "It is the way of his kind."

"He can't help it but that don' make it no better," said Ruby. "Now go to sleep."

Then she was quiet and in the background as he drifted off to sleep, Remo heard the drums begin again.

Generalissimo Corazon was in his long white night-gown when the two frightened guards were led into the presidential sitting room.

They prostrated themselves on the floor before him.

"It was the *duppies*," one of them wept. "Zombies."

"So you dropped your weapons and fled like children," Corazon said.

"They were coming for us," the other guard cried. "The drums stopped and then they came down the street at us and they had their arms up and they was coming for us."

"It was the voodoo. The zombies," the other guard tried to explain. "The evil power."

"The power, hah?" Corazon yelled. "I show you the power. I show you who gots the power, me or the voodoo. On your feet. Stand up."

He had the two men stand facing away from him and then took the drape off the mung machine and pressed the button. There was a loud crack, a zapping

159

noise, and as the two men melted into mush Corazon shouted again, "Now you see power. Real power. The power of Corazon. That be power."

Major Estrada stood on the side of the room quietly watching, noting that this time Corazon had pressed only one button to fire the machine and remembering which button it was.

"And don't you just be standing there, Estrada," Corazon called out. "You go get me some salt."

Estrada left and went to the kitchen of the palace where he took two saltshakers. One he put into his pocket and the other he brought back to Corazon, who sat in his gilt throne chair, looking glum.

Corazon took the shaker, looked at Estrada shrewdly, then unscrewed the top of the shaker and stuck his big index finger into the small jar. He tasted it to be sure it was salt. He nodded satisfaction.

"Now I got the salt, I all right," Corazon said. "The zombie, he can't live with the salt on him. And tomorrow I gonna go kill that Samedi, and I be the spiritual leader of this country forever and ever, amen." He gestured toward the spots on the floor. "And you, clean up that mess."

Remo awakened to the smell of food. It was a strange smell, one he could not place.

"'Bout time you get you lazy butt up," said Ruby working at a wood-fire stove in a corner of the shack's single room.

"Is Chiun awake yet?"

"He sleeping still, but he older than you. He got a right to sleep late and hanging 'round with you must give him lots of things to worry about and sleep off."

"What are you cooking? It smells awful," Remo

said. He flexed his muscles but realized with annoyance that the strength had not returned to them.

Ruby's voice rose in a piercing shriek. "Don't you worry about what it is. It put some flesh on you. You eat, you hear?" She was spooning food onto a plate. Watching her in her shapeless green dress, Remo could see the well-formed turn of her buttocks, the long line of thigh outlined by the material, the full, high breasts. He moved up into a sitting position on the cot.

"You know you'd be a good-looking woman if it wasn't for that hair of yours," he said. "It looks like something that was done by a high wind in a wheat field."

"Yeah, that's true," Ruby said thoughtfully. "But if I wore my 'fro, they recognize me around here for sure. This way is better, least till we be getting home. Here. Eat this."

She handed the plate to Remo, who examined it carefully. It was all vegetables—green stringy things and yellow stringy things. He had never seen any of them before.

"What is this? I'm not eating anything until I know what it is. I'm not eating any disguised neckbones or chitlins or like that," he said.

"It's just greens. You eat it." She began putting more on a plate for Chiun.

"What kind of greens?" Remo asked.

"What you mean, what kind of greens? It's greens. Greens be greens. What you need, a taster? Think you a king and somebody trying to poison you? You ain't no king, just a trouble-making turkey dodo fish-lip. Eat."

And because Remo feared that if he didn't Ruby

161

would turn her hundred-mile-an-hour earth-moving screech of a voice on him, he tasted some.

It wasn't too bad, he decided. And nourishment felt good in his body. He saw Chiun's eyes open. Ruby must have seen it too, because she was quickly at Chiun's side, cooing at the old man, helping him to sit up and gently but firmly planting a plate in his lap with orders to "eat this all up and don't leave none."

Chiun nodded and picked slowly at the food, but ate it all.

"I am not familiar with this food, but it was good," Chiun said.

Remo finished his, too.

"Good, there's more," Ruby said. "It put strength back in your bodies."

She refilled their plates, then sat on a low wooden footstool and watched them eat, as if she were counting their chews to make sure they didn't cheat.

When they were done, she stacked the plates on the stove, then went back to sit on her stool.

"I think we got to come to an agreement," she said.

Chiun nodded. Remo just looked at her.

"Now I'm taking charge here," she said.

Chiun nodded again.

"Why you?" asked Remo.

"Because I know what I'm doing," Ruby said. "Now you know I'm from the CIA. I don't know much about where you two are coming from, except it's something I probably don't wanna know about. But let's face it, you two just ain't much. I mean, you do a pretty good trick with that listening to people's feet so you know they carrying a gun, but what else do you do? You, dodo, you almost get yourself shot up by a guard and you bofe wind up in cages and Ruby's got to bail you out." She shook her head. "Not

162

much to talk about. Now I want to get outa here alive, so we do it my way. I gonna get rid of that Corazon and get somebody else running this place and we gonna get his machine and then we going back to America. That all right with you, old gentlemans?"

"His name is Chiun," Remo snapped. "Not 'old gentlemans.'"

"That all right with you, Mister Chiun?" Ruby asked.

"It is all right."

"Good," Ruby said. "Then it's agreed."

"Hey, wait a minute," said Remo. "What about me? You didn't ask me. Don't I count?"

"I don't know," Ruby said. "Let's hear you count."

"Aaah," Remo said in disgust.

"No, fish," said Ruby, "you don't count. You got nothin' to say about nothin'. And one thing more, when I get us all outa here—me and the old gentlemans, Mister Chiun—we got a deal about that learning how people are carrying guns, right?"

"Right," said Chiun. "Forty percent."

"Twenty," said Ruby.

"Thirty," said Remo.

"All right," Ruby said to Remo. She pointed to Chiun. "But he pays you outa his share. Maybe you get enough to buy yourself some new socks." She sniffed her disdain. "Country," she said.

"All right, Madam Gandhi. Now that you're in charge, you mind telling us how and when you're going to move against Corazon?"

"The how don't concern you, 'cause you just mess it up. The when is now. We already started. Eat some more greens."

163

"That's right, Remo. Eat some more greens," Chiun said.

Generalissimo Corazon had drafted the proclamation carefully. The old *hungan* had slipped through his fingers yesterday and the two Americans had escaped, but it did not matter. He had the mung machine and it worked against the Americans and it worked against the *hungan's* family. He had proved it yesterday when he had obliterated the high priest's son. So he had no fear any longer as he drafted the proclamation appointing himself "God for Life, Ruler Forever, President Eternal of All Baqia."

He came out on the steps of the palace leading to the courtyard to read it to his troops before he led them to the mountains to flush out the old voodoo leader, Samedi.

But where were the troops?

Corazon looked around the palace courtyard. There were no soldiers to be seen. He glanced upwards at the flagpole. Hanging from the rope beneath the Baqian flag was a stuffed dummy. It was dressed in a soldier's uniform and wore riding boots and had a chestful of medals. It was grossly overpadded and meant to represent Corazon. Hanging from its chest was a cloth sign. A breeze caught the pennant and floated it out straight, so Corazon could read the words:

"The *hungan* of the hills say Corazon will die. He is a pretender to the throne of Baqia."

Generalissimo Corazon dropped the proclamation on the stone steps and fled inside the palace.

CHAPTER TWELVE

It took four direct orders from Generalissimo Corazon
to get a soldier to climb the flagpole and take down
the dummy of the general and the threatening banner.

While he climbed, the drums began beating louder
and the soldiers in the guard posts around the palace
wall looked toward the hills in fear.

"Now burn it," Major Estrada said after the soldier
had cut the dummy loose, to fall on the ground, and
then slid back down the flagpole.

"Not me, Major," said the soldier. "Don't make me
do that."

"Why not?"

"'Cause I probably dead already for what I do.
Don't make me go burning no magic."

"There is no magic except El Presidente's magic,"
snapped Estrada.

"Good. Let El Presidente's magic remove the

dummy," the soldier said. "I will not." He picked up his rifle and walked back to his guard station.

Estrada scratched his head, then dragged the dummy to a maintenance room near the palace garage, where he threw it on a pile of garbage.

Corazon thanked Estrada for removing the effigy. The president sat in his throne room, the saltshaker tied about his neck on a leather thong.

"We going to get rid of that old *hungan* in the mountains," he said.

"Who's going to do it?" asked Estrada.

"Me. You. The army."

"They scared. You be lucky to get six soldiers to go with you."

"They're afraid of what?"

"You hear those drums getting louder? They peeing their pants," Estrada said.

"I got the machine."

"The machine is a month old," Estrada said. "They haven't had time to learn to be afraid of it. But they been afraid of these drums all their lives."

"We gonna go anyway and get that old man. Then nobody is left to challenge me. The Americans probably on their way home by now."

"When you going to go?" asked Estrada.

"*We* are going as soon as I decide to go," Corazon said. He waved Estrada away with his hand.

It was 9 A.M.

By 9:45 A.M., a new dummy of Generalissimo Corazon hung from the flagpole in the palace courtyard.

None of the guards had seen anybody lift the dummy up the flag rope. And none could explain how the body of Private Torrez, who had climbed the pole

166

to remove the first dummy, had gotten to the base of the flagpole.

Torrez was dead. His heart had been cut from his body.

This time no one would go up the flagpole to remove the manikin.

Estrada told this to Corazon, who came out onto the side steps of the palace and shouted:

"Hey, you, up there in the guard tower. Climb up that pole and get that dummy down."

The guard kept his back to Corazon and looked out over Ciudad Natividado.

"Hey, I calling you. Don't you hear me?"

The guard did not move a muscle to respond.

Corazon yelled orders to three other guards.

They ignored him.

And silence hung over the courtyard as Corazon stopped yelling, silence made deeper by the throbbing of the drums.

For the first time, Corazon looked at the dummy. It was another stuffed soldier's uniform, replete with medals imitating Corazon's fruit-salad chest.

A banner was tacked to the chest of this dummy, too. A dark cloud passed overhead, carrying a hint of rain and a puff of wind. It unfurled the banner.

The legend read:

"I wait for you today. At the pits. My power against your power."

Corazon screamed an anguished cry, compounded of hatred and annoyance and fear.

He turned to Estrada.

"Round up as many men as you can for this afternoon. We going up there to get rid of this man once and for all."

"Right, El Presidente," said Estrada. "Right."

Corazon went inside to wait.

When Remo awoke from his nap, he knew it was back. His breathing was low and slow, filling his lungs with air, and he could feel the oxygen coursing through his body, flooding his muscles with a quiet energy. His senses were sharp. As he had ever since arriving in Baqia he heard the drums, but he also heard children and an occasional vehicle and chickens. One chicken was having its neck wrung. A jeep went by, tapping the tune of a defective cylinder. Children were skipping rope nearby. The smell of vegetables was in the air, but Remo no longer had to wonder what Ruby had cooked for them. He smelled turnip greens and some kind of mustardy vegetable, and there was a faint cooking aroma of vinegar.

"Chiun," Remo called as he hopped up off his cot, "I'm back together again."

"Sheeit," came Ruby's voice. "Everybody watch theyselves now. He's back together again. As bad as new."

Ruby was sitting on her stool in front of Chiun's cot. Chiun was seated. They were playing dice on the sheet.

"Who's winning?" Remo asked.

"I do not understand this game," Chiun said.

"I'm winning," Ruby said. "Two hundred dollars."

Chiun was shaking his head. "If she rolls a seven, she wins. I roll a seven and I lose. This I do not understand."

"Just the way the rules are," Ruby said. "It's all right. I trust you for the money. Besides we got to stop now."

She came to Remo and whispered, "How's he do that?"

168

"Do what?"

"Roll a seven whenever he wants. They my dice, too."

"That's our business," Remo said. "We're gambling experts for the U.S. government. We came down here to open a luxury hotel and casino. We were going to open one in Atlantic City but we couldn't figure out who to bribe."

"Stop talking smart," Ruby said.

"Got any more greens?" Remo asked.

"You slept through lunch," Ruby said. "You slow, you blow."

"I'll show you how to roll the dice if you feed me," Remo bribed.

"We don't have time," Ruby said. "Besides, the greens all gone. Old gentlemans eat them all."

"Too bad. I'll show you what you're missing. Chiun, toss me the dice, please."

Ruby watched. Chiun held the two red dice in his right hand, looking at the white spots. He curled his long-nailed fingers, then propelled the dice from his palm. Faster than Ruby's eyes could follow, they sped across the ten feet of space between the two men, whirring.

Remo plucked them out of the air between his fingers, like a magician materializing a back-palmed card.

"Watch now," he said to Ruby. "I'll play you for ten dollars."

He shook the dice, called "Nine" and dropped the pair on the dirt floor. They hit, rolled, and turned up six and three.

Remo picked them up again. "Four," he said. "Hard way." He rolled the dice across the floor in a pair of twos.

He picked them up again. "Pick a number," he said. "Any number."

"Twelve," Ruby said.

Remo shook the dice and rolled a pair of sixes in the dirt.

"Twelve," he said proudly.

"Boxcars! You lose," Ruby shrieked. "Where's my ten dollars?"

Remo looked at her in astonishment. "Chiun. I know how you lost."

"How?"

"She cheated."

"You just a sore loser," Ruby said. "I collect later. Come on now, we got to go." As they went out the back door of the shack, Ruby told Remo, "I forget the ten dollars if you teach me to roll dice like that."

"Anybody can learn," Remo said.

"How long it take?"

"Average person, forty years, four hours a day. You, twenty years."

"Then it took you sixty years and you ain't that old. How you do it?" Ruby demanded.

She was leading them toward a pre-World War II green Plymouth that looked like a "speed kills" display by the National Safety Council.

"It's all feel," Remo said. "You feel the dice."

"I wanna know how you do it, not how you feel. You decide you going to tell me, you and me we can make a deal."

"I'll think about it," Remo said.

Ruby herded them into the car, started the motor, and drove off. She drove around the backs of shacks, avoiding children and chickens, until she was out of the main city. Then she cut through some barren flatland to get onto the main road. Remo noted approv-

170

ingly that she drove the old car expertly, not riding the clutch, shifting smoothly and changing gears at the precise moment to get the maximum power out of the old wreck.

"Mind telling us where we're going?" Remo asked.

"We gonna finish this all up now, so I can get home," Ruby said. "By the time I get back to my wig factory, those damn 'Bamas, they have theyselves a union and everything. This trip be costing me money." Her tone left no doubt that Ruby thought losing money was important.

"How are we going to finish it up?" Remo said.

"Correction. *I'm* going to finish it up. You going to watch. This no job for a dice tosser."

"How?" Remo insisted.

"We gonna overthrow Corazon and we gonna put a new man in. And we gonna get that machine of his and you going to take it back to Washington with you."

"You've got it all figured out," Remo said.

"Trust your old Ruby. And stay outa the way if things hot up, 'cause I don't wanna have to explain how I lost you."

"Are there any more home like you?" asked Remo.

"Nine sisters. You wanna get married?"

"Not unless they cook like you."

Ruby shook her head. "They wouldn't have you, anway. Except one of 'em, she kinda stupid, she maybe would take you."

"You know, you're the first CIA type I ever met who could cook," Remo said.

"Stop talking stuff to me," Ruby said. "You know I'm the first CIA type you ever met who knew how to do anything. But they pay on time."

"Hear, hear," called Chiun from the back seat. "You

171

see, Remo. This young lady knows what is important."

"You got trouble collecting from that Doctor Smith? He a tight and tired-ass-sounding old thing."

"Actually," Chiun said, "only Remo works for Smith. I work for the President. But Smith is supposed to pay us. He is awful. If I were not on him constantly, we would never get our stipend. And it is not nearly what we are worth."

"Well, maybe you," Ruby said, "but . . ." She nodded toward Remo.

"Chiun, knock it off," Remo said. "You get your pay all the time. You have it delivered by special submarine, for God's sake. And I don't notice you wanting for anything."

"Respect," Chiun said. "There are things, Remo, that money cannot buy. Respect."

Remo could tell by the way Ruby set her lips that she did not agree with Chiun, but wasn't prepared to argue it with him.

Ciudad Natividado was now far behind them. They were speeding along Route 1 toward the far-off hills. The dusty road was a meager two-lane strip cut through an overhang of jungle trees, so it seemed to Remo as if he were riding through a green tunnel. Even inside the car the sound of the drums was growing louder.

Remo heard a faint tapping sound and realized a light shower was falling. He was protected from it by the overhang of the trees.

Ruby noticed it, too. "Good," she said. "The old man told me it'd rain. We need that."

"Will someone please tell me what you're up to?" Remo asked exasperatedly.

"You'll see. We're almost there." She slowed down

and as she did she twisted in her seat to look behind her. Far behind were two cars.

"'Less I miss my guess, that be Corazon," Ruby said. "Right on time."

Ahead Remo saw the black pitch pit at the base of the hill. It seemed to be giving off steam. Ruby pulled the old Plymouth off the road through brush and past walls of vines and stumps until she was fifty feet from the road, as unseeable as an Alabama motorcycle cop hiding behind a billboard.

"Now you two wait here. And keep your little lips still, you," she told Remo. "We don' want nothin' going wrong."

She jumped from the car and a few moments later had vanished into the brush.

"That woman thinks I'm an idiot," Remo groused to Chiun.

"Hmmm," said Chiun. "The rain has stopped."

"Well?"

"Well, what?" asked Chiun.

"What do you think about her thinking I'm an idiot?" Remo demanded.

"Some are wise beyond their years."

Ruby met Samedi walking slowly down the hillside toward the pitch pit. He wore the same shirtless black trousers and bare feet, but for the occasion he wore a top hat and a white collar around his bare neck. In his hand he carried a long bone that looked like the thighbone of a human being.

"Hurry, holy one," Ruby said in Spanish. "Corazon is almost on us."

He glanced up at the sky. The sun was moving out from behind a gray cloud.

173

"The sun will shine," he said. "It is a good day for doing good works."

He followed Ruby down the hillside. She stopped ten feet from the tar pits, near a large rock outcropping.

"Here you must sit," she said.

He nodded and sank into a squatting position.

"You know what to do?" she said.

"Yes," he said. "I will know what to do to the murderer of my child and my land."

"Fine," said Ruby. "I will be near."

A few minutes later Ruby was back at the old Plymouth. The heavy roar of Corazon's limousine and a small backup jeep with four soldiers in it grew louder.

"Want to watch the fun?" Ruby asked.

"Wouldn't miss it," Remo said.

He and Chiun followed her to a break in the foliage from which they could peer out over the tar pit.

"Who's the old guy in the funny clothes?" asked Remo.

"He is Samedi," said Chiun, cautiously.

"How you know that?" piped Ruby. "I just found out yesterday his name's Samedi."

"Samedi is not a name, young woman. It is a title. He is leader of the undead."

"That mean zombies," Ruby explained to Remo.

"I know what it means."

"I see some of them walking around up there yesterday," she said, "and I don't know if they zombies or they just buzzing with something. But whatever they are, it was them that got you out of the cages."

"The zombie need not be evil," Chiun said. "He does the bidding of Samedi, the master, and if the master be good, the works be good."

"Well, this gonna be very good works. He gettin'

174

rid of Corazon for us," Ruby said. "Shush now, they here."

The black presidential limousine rolled up and slid to a smooth halt only a few feet from the pit of pitch. The jeep stopped behind it and four soldiers got out of the jeep and stood with their rifles across their chests.

Corazon got out the door of the limousine on Remo's side and hoisted the mung machine out in his big thick arms. His chauffeur and another guard, both carrying pistols, got out the front doors. After Corazon set the machine on the ground, Major Estrada slid across the seat and came out the same door.

Corazon looked toward the tar pit. He saw the old man sitting on the rock, no more than one hundred feet away.

A broad smile split Corazon's chocolate face.

He pushed the mung machine in front of him. Its wheels were too small to roll smoothly over the rough road surface and the machine bumped and skidded as Corazon guided it toward the edge of the black lake. The pitch spit heavy fumes into the air. Heat shimmered from its surface as the hot afternoon sun dried the small shower sprinkle of a few minutes before.

"Samedi, I am here," Corazon bellowed. "To match your magic against mine."

"Your magic is no magic at all," Samedi called back. "It is the trickery of a fool, an evil fool. That trickery soon will be with us no more."

"We will see," Corazon said. "We will see."

The sound of the drums grew louder. It seemed to infuriate Corazon, who hoisted the mung machine into his arms. He aimed carefully at Samedi, who sat motionless on the stone, then pressed the button.

There was a ripping sound and then a green dart of

light flashed out and splashed against the hill. But it missed Samedi by twenty feet.

"*Aaargghh*," screamed Corazon in enraged fury. He aimed the machine and fired again. Again he missed.

In the brush, Remo said, "He's taking dead aim. Why's he missing?"

"He is not seeing Samedi," Chiun explained. "The vapor from the tar is creating a mirage and he is firing at the vision he thinks he sees."

"Thass right," Ruby said.

Corazon took a deep breath. He aimed carefully and fired again. Behind him, his soldiers leaned on their rifles, watching. Major Estrada sat on the front fender of the limousine, his watchful eyes surveying everything.

Corazon's shot missed and this time the green glow was a weak pale shimmer.

"He's not giving it a chance to charge up," Remo said softly.

Corazon shouted and in a mad rage raised the mung machine over his head and tried to throw it at Samedi. But the heavy machine sailed only ten feet through the air, then landed on the lake of pitch with a dull plop. It lay there like the hull of a wrecked ship half-buried in sand at low tide.

"And now you have no magic at all," Samedi called out. He clapped his hands and rising from clumps of brush on the hillside as if they were instant blooming trees rose ten, twelve, twenty black men, wearing white trousers and no shirts, all with the glazed eyes that Remo had seen the night before in the two men who had walked down Ciudad Natividado's main street and terrified the guards.

"Attack," cried Samedi and the men raised their arms and began to shuffle down the hillside.

Corazon realized that he had thrown away his only true hope of staying in power. He grabbed a stick and leaned over the edge of the lake, trying to spear the mung machine and pull it back to him.

As he teetered on the edge, Major Estrada tossed away his cigarette, took a deep breath, then charged forward. His outstretched arms hit Corazon midrump and El Presidente went tumbling forward into the lake of pitch. The black goo sucked at him, pulling him partly down, and he shouted, but he was stuck there, like a fossil embedded in amber.

"I wasn't countin' on that," Ruby said.

Estrada turned to the soldiers. "Now we return to the real island magic," he shouted. "Fire on them. Raise those rifles. If you want to live, fire." He pointed toward Samedi.

The soldiers looked hesitant. The zombies now had split into two groups and were coming around the lake toward the soldiers.

Estrada reached into a pocket of his tunic and pulled out a cloth bag of salt. He drew a large circle on the ground with the white powder and called the soldiers.

"Come inside. The *duppies* cannot harm you here. And then we rid the island of this foolishness." He waved his arm and the soldiers moved up to join him.

Ten feet out in the lake Corazon had wrapped his arms around the mung machine and was screaming for help.

"Pull me out of here. Estrada, come get me."

"Sorry, Generalissimo," Estrada called. "I've got other things to do."

He grabbed the rifle of the nearest soldier and pushed it up to the soldier's shoulder. "Fire that

177

weapon," he ordered. He pulled his automatic pistol from his holster.

"They gonna get the old man," Ruby said.

Remo looked at Chiun.

"Since I don't work for the President and I'm only here as a spectator, Chiun, what do you think?" he said.

"I think you are absolutely right," Chiun said.

And before Ruby could speak, Chiun and Remo had leaped from the ground and sliced their way through the heavy brush as if it were not there.

The soldiers had their rifles to their shoulders and were all aiming at Samedi. Estrada's finger was tightening on the trigger when Remo and Chiun hit the circle of salt.

Before Ruby's wondering eyes the bodies of khaki-clad soldiers began flying through the air. She saw Remo and Chiun moving through the seven men so slowly that it looked as if any one of the soldiers could have felled them just by swinging his rifle. But where the soldiers grabbed, Chiun and Remo had just vacated. They moved strangely, fast without seeming to hurry, intensely without seeming to strain for power, and the air was filled with the thwacks of blows and the cracking of bones and the screaming of soldiers. The two men's hands were blurs.

In ten seconds it was over and the seven soldiers lay in the dirt, Major Estrada face-down, his hand still wrapped tightly around his pistol butt, but his trigger finger removed from his hand.

Now the zombies were around the lake and moving toward Remo and Chiun.

Remo saw them and said, "I wasn't exactly counting on this, Little Father. Quick. How do you kill the already dead?"

Before Chiun could answer, Samedi rose to his feet from the rock. He clapped his hands and the twenty men stopped as if they were automatons, all fired from a single power source that had just been turned off.

"*Wowee*," Ruby said. She rose up from the brush and joined Remo and Chiun in the roadway.

"How you do that? Hah? How you do that?" she asked Remo in a high screech.

"Ruby," Remo explained patiently, "shut up."

As Samedi came walking slowly around the lake of pitch men and women appeared on the plateau atop the hill, looking down, watching.

Generalissimo Corazon had sunk halfway into the tar, but with a mighty effort he turned himself half on his side, still holding onto the mung machine.

"You will never rule, Samedi," he shouted. "I have the power. Me. Corazon."

Samedi ignored him.

Corazon wrapped his arms around the mung machine, searching for the firing switch. He found it and squeezed. But the machine was aimed in the wrong direction. There was a sharp crack and then a green glow enveloped Generalissimo Corazon as the machine fired point-blank into his stomach, and he seemed illuminated for a split second before he turned into a green ooze that settled onto the surface of the lake. His cotton uniform vanished and all that was left to mark the remains of God for Life, Ruler Forever, President Eternal of All Baqia were his golden medals, which floated momentarily on the green puddle and then vanished into the lake of pitch as the mung machine sank under the surface with a sucking gulp that pulled down the medals, the nails from his riding boots, and the green puddle that had been Corazon.

"Return," Samedi barked out and the twenty men with glazed eyes turned away and began to shuffle back toward the hillside, toward the village.

Samedi stopped in front of Ruby, Remo, and Chiun.

"Now what, child?" he asked Ruby.

"You be the leader," Ruby said. "It's up to you to run Baqia."

"I am old for leadership," Samedi said.

"A mere boy," said Chiun, his eyes on a level with Samedi's. "You have many years. And I am authorized by my employer, who is the President of the United States himself, because I do not work for minions, to tell you that the United States will give you all the help you need."

"Thank you," said Samedi. "But I don't even know where to start."

"Start by killing one hundred and fifty suspected traitors," Chiun said.

"Why?" asked Samedi.

"It's good form. Everybody does it."

"We didn't get the machine," Ruby groused on the plane back to the States that night.

"Neither did anybody else," said Remo. "It's gone. Let's forget it."

"CIA crazy sometimes. I probably gonna get fired," Ruby said. "Gonna lose that check."

"Don't worry. Chiun'll put in a word for you with his employer. In case you're the only person in the world who hasn't heard it yet, he works for the President of the United States."

"No more," said Chiun.

180

"Oh?" asked Remo. "Why not? You mean you're coming back to join us peons working for Smith?"

"Why not?" said Chiun, his voice quivering with outrage. "Did you see my message of congratulations today when all was accomplished?"

"No," said Remo.

"Neither did I. I will not work for ingrates," Chiun said. "At least with Smith, you expect him to be a lunatic."

"True, Little Father. True. And what are you going to do, Ruby?"

"I going back to my wig factory and try to make ends meet. And then you gonna show me some of them tricks, like seeing the guns and rolling the dice and all."

Remo leaned close to her. "I'll tell you everything if you just go to bed with me."

Ruby laughed. "What I want with you? I already got a goldfish. You know," she said, "you ain't half-bad."

Remo smiled.

"No. You all bad," she said. "The old gentleman's going to show me."

"Forty percent," said Remo.

"Twenty," said Ruby.

"Thirty," said Chiun. "And I pay the dodo."

THE EXECUTIONER
by Don Pendleton

#1:	WAR AGAINST THE MAFIA	(17-024-3, $3.50)
#2:	DEATH SQUAD	(17-025-1, $3.50)
#3:	BATTLE MASK	(17-026-X, $3.50)
#4:	MIAMI MASSACRE	(17-027-8, $3.50)
#5:	CONTINENTAL CONTRACT	(17-028-6, $3.50)
#6:	ASSAULT ON SOHO	(17-029-4, $3.50)
#7:	NIGHTMARE IN NEW YORK	(17-066-9, $3.50)
#8:	CHICAGO WIPEOUT	(17-067-7, $3.50)
#9:	VEGAS VENDETTA	(17-068-5, $3.50)
#10:	CARIBBEAN KILL	(17-069-3, $3.50)
#11:	CALIFORNIA HIT	(17-070-7, $3.50)
#12:	BOSTON BLITZ	(17-071-5, $3.50)
#13:	WASHINGTON I.O.U.	(17-172-X, $3.50)
#14:	SAN DIEGO SIEGE	(17-173-8, $3.50)
#15:	PANIC IN PHILLY	(17-174-6, $3.50)
#16:	SICILIAN SLAUGHTER	(17-175-4, $3.50)
#17:	JERSEY GUNS	(17-176-2, $3.50)
#18:	TEXAS STORM	(17-177-0, $3.50)

WARBOTS by G. Harry Stine

#5 OPERATION HIGH DRAGON   (17-159, $3.95)

Civilization is under attack! A "virus program" has been injected into America's polar-orbit military satellites by an unknown enemy. The only motive can be the preparation for attack against the free world. The source of "infection" is traced to a barren, storm-swept rock-pile in the southern Indian Ocean. Now, it is up to the forces of freedom to search out and destroy the enemy. With the aid of their robot infantry—the Warbots—the Washington Greys mount Operation High Dragon in a climactic battle for the future of the free world.

#6 THE LOST BATTALION   (17-205, $3.95)

Major Curt Carson has his orders to lead his Warbot-equipped Washington Greys in a search-and-destroy mission in the mountain jungles of Borneo. The enemy: a strongly entrenched army of Shiite Muslim guerrillas who have captured the Second Tactical Battalion, threatening them with slaughter. As allies, the Washington Greys have enlisted the Grey Lotus Battalion, a mixed-breed horde of Japanese jungle fighters. Together with their newfound allies, the small band must face swarming hordes of fanatical Shiite guerrillas in a battle that will decide the fate of Southeast Asia and the security of the free world.

#7 OPERATION IRON FIST   (17-253, $3.95)

Russia's centuries-old ambition to conquer lands along its southern border erupts in a savage show of force that pits a horde of Soviet-backed Turkish guerrillas against the freedom-loving Kurds in their homeland high in the Caucasus Mountains. At stake: the rich oil fields of the Middle East. Facing certain annihilation, the valiant Kurds turn to the robot infantry of Major Curt Carson's "Ghost Forces" for help. But the brutal Turks far outnumber Carson's desperately embattled Washington Greys, and on the blood-stained slopes of historic Mount Ararat, the high-tech warriors of tomorrow must face their most awesome challenge yet!